Beatrice

ANNEMARIE BREAR

Cover images by AM Brear, BookBrush

For Kat

Beatrice

Hello Readers,

Before you begin reading this book, I must tell you about its history.

My dear friend Kathryn, a fellow writer, and I met way back in 2001 on an online critique group for writers. Kat, American, me Australian. Kat adored all things Regency, and my passion was the Victorian era. At this time, I was still four years away from signing with an agent and becoming published.

We became instant writing buddies, but didn't like the group, so we thought to start our own online critique group for historical fiction writers. Everything was done online. We'd chat all day, nearly every day, on MSN. Our chat box would be up on screen for most of the day, but we'd do our thing — writing, eating, drinking, housework, etc – and come back to chat when we had something to share. We shared our lives all via a chat box and the odd phone call when the time difference allowed. (It was Kat who taught me what LOL and brb meant way back when they were first invented.) We each had a MySpace, and then in 2007 we each joined Facebook when it became the 'in' thing to be on.

Both Kat and I strived to be published; it was our dream. Through sheer determination, I managed to keep sending out manuscripts, kept posting wads of paper bound in rubber bands to publishing houses and to agents' desks around the world.

Kat didn't have the same confidence. She wouldn't submit her stories; always said they needed more work. I disagreed, for her Regency stories were brilliantly written, but I let her travel her own path and supported her when I could.

Then her health began to deteriorate – it became her main focus.

Years passed, and Kat watched my children grow up and congratulated me on becoming a grandparent. My writing career flourished while Kat kept her unfinished works hidden away.

Around the 2010s she finally had a short story published, Eightball, a modern romance. I helped her achieve that one small goal. Next, I wanted to guide her through getting her Regency novels finished.

To keep her momentum going, we decided to write a story together of the same female character - Beatrice. Kat would write the younger Regency Beatrice, and I would write the older Victorian Beatrice. We were writing to our strengths.

Over the next six months or so, we would send each other emails with each day's diary entry.

However, life has a way of sending curveballs. Fate intervened, and Kat's health suffered even more, and I became far too busy with writing my own novels, and so Beatrice was sidelined, unfinished, in a messy state of bits and pieces, blank pages and making little sense.

The years trickled by as Kat focused on her health and the body that was letting her down. She loved politics and would message me about certain leaders, complaining of their inefficiency. I had no interest in American politics, but I'd listen and agree that the world was going mad. Kat had clear convictions on many subjects, was terribly intelligent, enjoyed researching historical facts and loved her cats (I'm a dog person) but she could also be so very funny. She made me laugh so much.

Around 2016, Kat and I were talking on Messenger, and she was in ill health but determined to work on some of her Regency stories. I quipped that we should finish Beatrice, but she wanted to work on one of her stories instead. She wasn't even sure she still had her copies of Beatrice's diary entries as she'd had computer crashes over the years and lost a great deal of files. I managed to find a copy of Beatrice on an old USB. I put all the separate diary entries into one document.

We had every intention of finishing it. One day.

It didn't happen. Life got in the way again.

I moved countries twice, remarried, and began writing full-time as my career blossomed.

Kat never married and lived with her mother, and money was tight. For years she fought sickness and ill health, and in December 2024, I was sent the news that sadly she had died. I was heartbroken. I'd lost a dear friend of over 23 years' standing.

On the first anniversary of Kat's death, I decided to re-read the diary entries. Goodness, what a mess they were in. We'd never done any editing on it. It was a raw compilation of dates, names, blank pages, unfinished paragraphs, and a vague idea to make it all make sense. I went back through our messenger chats to see if there were any files missing, but reading Kat's comments made me miss her. I put Beatrice away, unsure what to do about the diary entries.

I gave it a few weeks and then I brought out the file again and was determined to make it good, to honour Kat.

I deleted all the blank pages with just dates written on them and concentrated on the pages that actually had text. I started making notes (a great many notes) of everything Kat had written, but many of her entries were unfinished, so I had to tap into her writing style (ridiculously difficult) and finish what she wrote, or changed things to make sense, believing I knew her well enough to know what she meant for that particular entry.

Next was the editing. I have tried to keep to Kat's style of writing of how a young woman of that era would write, with the odd capitalisations, etc, and keeping the tone of how they spoke and thought, but Kat did her research so thoroughly and was such a purest that she wrote original words of the period which would confuse the readers and she also wrote with the old English Regency spelling which again would pull the reader out of the story. So, reluctantly, I had to edit or rewrite the text to match the modern readers' expectations.

Then came the formatting, which was a complete mess as the entries were written on old versions of Word or copied from previous old email programs. It took a long time, hours, and days of sorting out each entry.

The end result is that in this book the Regency part of the diary ends abruptly, because that's where Kat stopped writing it and I didn't want to write fresh entries in her style. I felt there was enough of the younger Beatrice written for the reader to know the girl before she became a woman.

The Victorian part, my part, took more work as I had to complete my own diary entries to complete the story in a satisfying way.

This project of pulling it all together was a labour of love. It was hard work, long hours, but I felt I needed to do it. I didn't really do it for the readers (I hope you forgive me) because it was never started for readers. Writing Beatrice was a project between Kat and I for our own amusement, really. It was started as a way to keep Kat occupied while she dealt with doctor's appointments and being housebound.

I wasn't going to publish this book, and simply keep it to myself, or perhaps make a copy to give to Diane, Kat's mother, until I found out Diane had died in late 2025. Then a little voice in my head — *maybe it was Kat's* — said publish it, let people read/hear her Regency voice at last, even if it's only in little diary entries.

So, I have done. I hope you enjoy it readers.

Kat, I hope I have made my dear friend proud.

With love,

AnneMarie.

Beatrice

The diary of a young lady during the Regency era and then a later diary when Beatrice is an older woman in the Victorian era.

10 May, 1820

My first entry in this precious book must be of praise to the generosity of my family. It has been such a Delightful day. I am now *Out* as Mother calls it. Today I turned Seventeen! Miss Horace (governess) gave me this book to record my thoughts. Mama had Powers, her maid, cut my hair in the latest fashion, straight from La Belle Assemblée. Papa gave me twenty guineas to buy myself a new dress and fripperies from the milliner. The emerald ribbons have spoken to me quite firmly when I have gone with mother to Mrs Dawsons. I will use it to re-trim my bonnet and update my best dress.

Little Cordelia (Delia) gave me a dozen handkerchiefs painstakingly stitched with my initials. Mama assures me that my brothers will send me something from their respective schools, but David never remembers to write me now that he is occupied at Oxford. And poor Samuel at Rugby rarely has a farthing to spend on anyone but himself.

I saved a lock from my formerly waist-length hair. No longer. I miss it already, for my head feels so light I think it could float away.

Tonight, I ate with Papa and Mama instead of in the nursery with Delia. Tomorrow I will be attending dinner at the Vicar's. I look in the mirror and cannot see the changes. Perhaps tomorrow when I wake up, they will make themselves known. Seventeen! Seems a grand age to be. Molly will be attending me each morning to help me dress and tend my clothes. No more must I share the nursemaid with my sister.

Mama says I must continue my lessons with Miss Horace on the pianoforte, and she has hired a dancing master to practise with me so that I may be proficient when I attend my first assembly. It is but three weeks away. I am dreadfully excited and cannot wait for the day to come.

Papa let me have one glass of Champagne with which they saluted my anniversary. I did not like the first sip, I sneezed at the second and fell quite in love with it by the third. Dinner was richly dressed with French sauces. And for our celebration, there were many cakes and sweetmeats set upon our table. Lemon cakes, Orange Tarts, Macaroons.

I am so very tired from all the excitements of the day, but do not want it to end and so cannot bear to put my head to my pillow for fear of seeing it end. Molly is knocking on the door and wishes entry, so I must end this now. I have a special place I will hide you so no one will find you and may not read my thoughts.

Goodnight sweet diary.

11 May, 1820

Oh, it is good to be a woman grown! I can barely write for my fluttering emotions. Our dinner with Mr Wynchester, the Vicar, and his wife was enlivened by the presence of a gentleman of the most personable nature. Mr Cole Huntingdon, I sigh just to say his name. A most attractive name and ever so fitting of his noble features and manner. I must write it all now before any of it fades from my memory.

We arrived at the Vicar's House to a fulsome welcome. *"Mr Acherton and Lady Emma,"* Mr Wynchester greeted my parents graciously. *"Miss Acherton."* He smiled down at me with the most generous condescension. "Please let me make you known to my godson, Mr Huntingdon. He has been kind enough to make a stop on his way back to London." He was buying a horse from the Thorne farms and is expected back in the City for his mother's dress ball. I do so wish to attend a fancy-dress ball now that I am out. *"I am delighted to make your acquaintance."* Mr Huntingdon bowed to my father and over my mother's hand. When he turned to me, I could barely raise my eyes as he greeted me. Such distinguished looks and so charming a manner.

I was his partner for dinner, much to my pleasure. I could not find a word to say at first. But his gentle manner as he spoke so kindly to me put me at ease before the second course. I do not remember a word I said, but I remember his replies, which expressed such polite interest in my every utterance. I long to see him again. I do hope he will make a formal call upon us on the morrow. I equally hope that he will not consider departing for the City until he has had time to fully acquaint himself with our salubrious neighbourhood. I know I shall dream of him tonight, sweet diary, for all my thoughts revolve around him.

12 May, 1820

He came! He is the sweetest, kindest, most gentlemanly man I have ever been acquainted with. He brought me a posy of wildflowers. Exquisite Marsh Gentian, the same shade as my eyes he told me. I did not tell him of the spots of mud on his Hessians, I'm sure he would have been quite embarrassed to have missed the evidence of his labours. He stayed the full length allowed for a visit and showed every reluctance to leave when he must. He asked me to take a drive with him tomorrow. Diary, tomorrow cannot come soon enough. The remains of the day were sadly flat after he left. I did little but mending and some needlepoint, besides my lessons with Miss Horace.

The dancing master arrives on Monday. Little Delia will also take lessons; Papa considers it sensible to teach two rather than one.

I wish Mr Huntingdon would not be leaving so soon, so that he might claim a dance with me at the upcoming Assembly. I have a sneaking fear I will be left a wallflower.

13 May, 1820

It rained, it poured, it flooded. My hopes were dashed. Mr Huntingdon's groom brought a note of apology and a request to have my company on a day with better weather. I pined, I moped, I languished. Miss Horace told me I put forward no focus to my lessons. It was true; I could not play a note without thinking of him.

For dinner, we had Saddle of Mutton roasted, Potatoes, Colli-Flower-Broccoli, and Cucumber, Macaroni, sweet batter Pudding, and my favourite Raspberry Puffs. I ate three before Mother's frowns discouraged me from eating more. Cordelia was allowed to come down after dinner and join us.

We played lottery tickets, she and I, while Papa and Mama watched us indulgently. After Miss Horace took Cordelia up to bed, Mama read from Miss Austen's *Persuasion*. Mama feels her novels are far above others published today. I do agree they are delightful but do enjoy reading others. Miss Horace is kind enough to lend me her copies before she sends them back to the circulating library. The sun came out just before dusk, and I anticipate the weather will continue to improve. Tomorrow, I hope to see Mr Huntingdon at church.

14 May, 1820

Hanby drove us in the Landau to church this morning for the service. I barely heard a word of Mr Wynchester's sermon, for my eyes could not be torn from the back of Mr Huntingdon's blue superfine jacket. I had a fine opportunity to admire his brown hair, the colour of dark honey. He stood so straight and tall I could not help but sigh.

The Blacksmith's son was christened, and prayers for our new King were made. This is all I remember of my time in church today.

Outside the church, Mr Huntingdon, with polite graciousness, took his leave of us, though when he spoke aside to me for several minutes before Hanby brought forth our carriage, he assured me he would be back soon. I was delighted to hear this and have visions of us dancing at the assembly. I count down the days with great eagerness.

The afternoon and evening were quiet.

Mother read from the Bible to us, and Cordelia recited her passages she had been set to memorise. She did very well and received much praise from our parents. I think sometimes that they love her best, for truly she is the smartest and prettiest of us.

She is said to take after our grandmother, who was the daughter of a Duke and very prideful of that fact.

I wish I too, like my grandmother Acherton, could take London by storm. We may go to London this summer for the King's coronation. I cannot wait to see the city in all its splendour. Someday I will be able to tell my children of such a glorious sight.

Mother reminded me to be downstairs early tomorrow in expectation of the arrival of Mr LaRue, the dancing master.

15 May, 1820

I am so tired, I can hardly keep from yawning.

I do not like the Dance Master's hands. They are damp and hold me too tight. Miss Horace played the latest airs as Mr LaRue attempted to teach Delia and I the latest dances. Waltzes, Quadrilles, Cotillions, as well as the many country dances. Some we knew, but he insisted we both be steppe perfect by the end of the day. My feet are sore, and my person assaulted by his seeming familiarity. I do not know whether I should tell my mother. Perhaps it would be best to let the tutoring run its course and allow him to leave as planned. I do not believe either Miss Horace or Cordelia noticed anything wrong. Could I be imagining it? I do not think I would mind if it were Mr Huntingdon holding me so tightly.

Already I long to see Mr Huntingdon again. I can wish for nothing but this week to pass quickly.

Mama went into Newbury. I wish to have gone with her. She brought back with her the most delightful fabric, and this will make my dress for the Assembly. Mama has let me choose the style from a recent issue of La Belle Assemblée, and Mrs Edding will come to take my measurements tomorrow.

Dinner today was very pleasant. Miss Horace joined us, and Papa paid me special attention today. He told me I am looking very pretty and grown up and asked if I was progressing with my piano lessons. Miss Horace complimented my performance and told him I was a natural and graceful dancer. Papa left us after dinner. Miss Horace returned to her rooms, leaving Mama and I alone. I almost then told her about Mr LaRue, but she seemed much preoccupied. She did not speak much but to compliment my latest stitchwork.

16 May, 1820

I was so looking forward to the dance lessons; now I long for them to end. Mr LaRue said the most impertinent things to me. I tried to tell Miss Horace, but she was wholly obtuse and incapable of understanding me. It was not his words so much as the manner he used in speaking to them. All the while his hands were most familiarly grasping me as we danced. I've begged Delia not to move more than three feet from me during our lessons, but I do not see how she'll be able to prevent him from his horribly caressing ways.

Mother and Father had dinner with friends in Newbury, so I had dinner in the Nursery with Delia. We played lottery tickets after eating and then Miss Horace read to us from Bowlder's Family Shakespeare. I've snuck into the library more than once to check passages she has read to us against the large leather-bound copy father has. So many of the words are as foreign as if they were Mohawk. But sometimes, I find the missing passage and understand what it is Mr Bowlder cut from the original. I think some of the words cut are of the same intent as Mr LaRue.

I wish it were Mr Huntingdon holding me so close, and whispering to me, but not, I think, what Mr LaRue speaks. I count the days until his return.

I have asked Molly to sleep in my dressing room for the next few nights, and though she looked at me oddly, she agreed. I feel safer somehow having her here. I think, I will perhaps be able to sleep tonight. I'll just have Molly lock the door.

17 May, 1820

I should not glory in another person's discomfort, but today I did. David arrived home today, fresh from University. He even remembered to bring me a Birth Day present. A very pretty beaded reticule stuffed with farthings. But it was later when he gave me my true present.

We were practising dancing and Mr LaRue, despite my attempts to keep Delia close, was becoming more and more impertinent. I was ready to slap him and report his behaviour to Mother when David seemed to appear from nowhere. He whirled me out of Mr LaRue's grasping arms and danced me around the room. When Mr LaRue protested his interruption, David said with the utmost haughtiness of his 19 years that Mr LaRue would satisfy himself with instructing me and partnering Delia. Mr LaRue stuttered and stammered in response but gave in with ill grace.

I did not know my brother was such a good dancer. Suddenly the lessons seemed so easy. I stopped stepping on toes and found I was good at dancing. Under David's watchful eye, Mr LaRue said no more than a half dozen words to me. Corrections only. I spoke to Delia later, and from her recounting of their partnering, it does not appear he tried anything resembling the liberties he was taking with me.

David spoke to me after and asked about Mr LaRue's manner. Upon hearing that today was not the first time Mr LaRue had been so forward, he chastised me for not speaking to our parents in one breath and expressing sympathy for my situation in the next. Graciously, he has agreed to attend all remaining lessons. David has promised to *"give him a leveller"* if Mr LaRue steps out of line again.

Dinner tonight was very festive with the addition of David at the table. He kept us quite amused as he told us tales from school. His friends sound a very rowdy group. After dinner, Mother and I left Father and David to their Port. Mother asked me how the dance lessons were progressing, and it was with relief I was able to tell her they were going very well.

Mother presented me with a set of pearls this evening. She said her mother gave them to her for her first dance. They are very lovely, exquisite in shade and of amazing regularity in size. She informed me we would be going into the village tomorrow to have a fitting for my new ball dress. I may also buy a new pair of gloves and stockings for the Assembly. I also want to buy some new ribbons to re-dress my bonnet with the farthings from David's present.

This morning, I woke with a sense of dread, and tonight am going to bed with a sense of contentment. I know I will sleep well tonight.

18 May, 1820

Mr LaRue has been sent off, David convinced Mama that his services were no longer required. I understand that the Herrons have hired him for a day of lessons, and so have the Buckminsters, though why they would need the lessons when they spend most of their months in London, I do not know.

David took me out to the kennels to see the new pups. Beautiful greyhounds so elegant already. The smallest nibbled the trim from my skirt, and I spent the evening repairing it. Little Misty, as David decided to name the smallest bitch pup, has come to stay with us. Mama did not approve entirely, but she has always had little strength against my brother's wiles. He slipped Misty into my room, and she sleeps at my feet as I write this.

19 May, 1820

Molly was horrified at the damage one small puppy could do in one night. My bed hangings were frayed by the batting of a reckless paw, my slippers were chewed to pieces, and a puddle was left by a chair. It seemed to me the small beast had spent the night on my bed, but it would appear this was not so. Misty has been banished from my room. David has reclaimed her with beguiling charm that drew Molly out of her black humour.

Mother had Delia and I show her our steps. David and Papa were impressed into partnering us. Delia was delighted by the attention from her Papa. He told her how pretty she looked in her sprigged muslin gown and complimented her fine skill with the latest steps. She blossomed from the usually awkward girl she can't help being at the age of twelve to the young woman she will be in a few more years.

I can see she will be prettier than I by far. She has Mother's delicate features, whilst I have Papa's more sturdy features. My nose will never be that fine, delicate shape, nor my mouth curve in a perfect bow. I do not repine. I consider my eyes fine and could wish to be taller, but alas that is not my fate.

After dinner, David and I performed our favourite songs for

our parents, who praised us as if they had not heard them before a hundred times. David's voice is so pleasant to listen to — a fine tenor to counterbalance my soprano.

It rained just before we went to bed. I can smell the freshness on the breeze as it creeps through the gap in the window. Molly does not approve of fresh air, but tonight it was warm enough to merit a small influx of air.

20 May, 1820

Today was the final fitting for my gown. It is so beautiful I want to wear it every waking minute. The silk is so smooth and soft I can barely keep my fingers from it. It is of the palest green, the hem bordered with grass green trim, and the belt is of a matching green with gold picked out in an embroidery so elaborate it looks to be jacquard. Pearls are sewn throughout the hem trim and matching sleeve trim. And Mother has made a garland with pearls for my hair to match my new necklace and the earring drops Mother is loaning me. We still need to find a pair of gloves and shoes to match this glorious costume.

David told me the most mischievous tales from school. Sometimes being a boy sounds so freeing and exciting. Sammy will be home any day now, and it will be good to see him again. He grew so much last year between the beginning and end of terms. I know not if I will recognise him. Already he is nearly as tall as I, and he is but ten. It is expected that he will outstrip David in height in a few more years. The greyhound pup has been sent to the kitchen, as it chewed a pair of David's best Hessian boots. As well as a pair of evening slippers. He will need to have new ones made for the Assembly dance.

Dinner tonight, Fillet of Veal roasted. Cod's head and shoulders, boiled, Oyster sauce. We had dried apples, Beefans. Mama let me have a little Port as she felt I looked peaked. Suddenly, I am very tired.

21 May, 1820

I spent the day in bed, ill. Molly came in to wake me and, noticing me restless and feverish, she went to Powers, who roused my mother. Mother insisted I not leave my bed; she was determined to apply leeches if I did not show any improvement by dinnertime. Blessedly, I did. I cannot help but dislike those horrid creatures attached to my flesh!

David snuck into my room midday and brought Misty with him. Though I had to keep her still and silent under my bedcovers when Mama came to check on me, I was pleased to have the company. It was a dreadfully boring day. I was not allowed to read; several unpleasant potions were poured down my throat by Powers or Molly, and so I slept.

By evening though I no longer had a fever, I did have a megrim, which I did not mention to anyone for fear of another day in bed. Mother gave me a glass of port to drink down a few minutes ago and told me to sleep. Therefore, I felt safe in slipping from my bed and writing this entry.

22 May, 1820

Mama allowed me from bed today. I was able to sit on the Recamier with a throw covering my legs. Miss Horace read to me several times during the day, for my amusement, and Delia was allowed to come talk to me. David snuck in and was chastised by Mama for *"exciting the invalid."*

Sally, the housemaid, came to stoke the fire the second time David snuck in, this time with Misty, and I do believe the girl is as forward as Mother has had cause to complain. The girl was making blatant sheep eyes at David. I did not tell Mama but wonder if I should.

Broth and Port were my dinner. I was very hungry by evening, but Mama thought it would not be good for me. David snuck me in some wonderful cakes and biscuits before he went to bed. I am nibbling them while I write this and ever so glad to have my big brother.

Misty is playing with the curtain tassel on my bed, and its wretched state will no doubt give Molly fits.

I am determined to be up tomorrow. I need to take a walk; my legs, I think, have forgotten how. I wish to smell the flowers I saw blooming from the Parlour window. I wish to visit Nutmeg, who must think I have forgotten her. I long to ride against the wind, to feel her speed as she dashes across the meadow. It has been four days since I have ridden her. How is it possible? Tomorrow will come faster if I go to sleep. So, sleep I will.

23 May, 1820

Tuesday

I rose early and was from bed before Mother had a chance to determine a need for me to remain in bed. I slipped into David's room with Misty to return her before Molly found her. Oh my, I cannot tell what I saw. It was... It was Shocking!!! I must tell, but not here. If Mother were to find such a thing, to know I saw such things, would horrify her. I will include it on a separate sheet, which can be hid in my secret spot.

After breakfast, I rode out on Nutmeg and David on her brother, Coriander. It was only then that I told him what I saw. I asked him to explain his actions, and he did, though in the most vague terms. I know a lady should not be curious, but I was. I pressed for more information and, with persistence, was rewarded.

Dinner was a quiet affair. Mother and Father were distracted by news from London. And I could not look at David without wanting to exclaim. I could not speak for the questions, the amazement, the perturbation knowledge gave me. I know how Eve felt after eating the apple. I went to bed early at Mother's encouragement.

Addendum

(WHAT I SAW THIS MORNING...)

I walked into David's room this morning and was most astonished by the sight of Sally, the housemaid, bouncing up and down upon my brother. Her skirts were bunched about the waist and her bodice undone. What I could see of David was quite bare. His hands were on Sally's... her bosom and the most agonised groans were issuing from both of them between laboured breaths. I stood stunned, holding Misty quite tightly until I heard her whimper. I loosened my hold, and she jumped to the floor. Neither Sally nor David noticed us. I stood for several moments longer trying to understand what I was seeing until sense told me it was not something for my eyes.

Later, David explained to me that this was what men and women did. I was shocked, for Sally is quite five years older than him, and they are not married. David explained that the lower classes have these animal passions and Sally had come to his room and made herself available to him.

I do not understand how he can find her handsome; she is quite blowsy in appearance, and her manners are crude. He told me that she had charms not apparent to my eye, but he did blush as he said it.

I know Mother would not approve of this, but I cannot bear to tattle on him. I cannot think his behaviour wise.

I wonder if I might discover a way to encourage Sally to take a new position in another household. I wonder if a small tale to Mrs Girling would be recommended. I will have to think on this and hope bad things do not happen in the meantime.

24 May, 1820

Wednesday

I have the most horrid megrim from my silent fury. I took Sally aside to speak to her about her behaviour. She spoke to me in the most base and pert manner. I am resolved to speak to Mother. Her manner has put her quite beyond the pale. *The words she said,* I do not know exactly what they mean, but I know they are bad. It would be horrible if she ruined David with her wiles.

The weather was poor today, windy in the morning and raining in the afternoon. I was quite impatient to be outside, but instead I was left to watch the flowers wilt under the weight of the rain.

Dinner was Veal and Roast Chicken, Greens, and Damson Tarts of which I ate little.

25 May, 1820

Thursday

I was on my way to speak with Mother when David pulled me aside. I do not know how he deduced what I intended. He begged me not to inform upon Sally and took the blame for their behaviour on himself. It was noble of him, for I know she is to blame. But his repeated entreaties on this issue, in the end, won my silence. In exchange, I received a pledge from him to forgo any further attentions to or from Sally. I feel slightly less worried now, for he would never break his promise.

We went riding today. I won the race to the Horse Chestnut tree and gained a forfeit. I plan to hold the forfeit for future use. I know there will be a time I will need it.

The wind picked up around dinnertime, and it is now raining quite fiercely. Dinner was fresh Salmon with Tench and Eel. I do not much like fish. Mother says I will learn to like it as I get older. Rump of Beef Stewed, Carrots and Peas, of which I'm quite fond.

After Dinner we had 2 Dishes of Strawberries, blanched Almonds with Raisins and Apples.

26 May, 1820

Friday

Very little happened today. I did not see Sally all day for it was her day off. Molly has been taking lessons from Powers and tried a new style with my hair. It was hideous, but I did not want to tell her and hurt her feelings. Delia and I practised duets with the latest music from London. She has a very pretty voice. But I will say I play the piano with greater ability than she. And not just because I am older. She does not have the patience for practising the fingering, whereas my fingers seem to find the keys with ease.

Delia has taken a fondness for a barn cat, but cannot persuade mother to let the beast in. Mother is horrified at the thought of the fleas that infest it. Delia keeps coming back covered in hay and dirt. Mother had restricted her to her room except for lessons and meals in the nursery. We continue practising our dancing. We take turns with the lead. Mother assures me that dancing with a man shorter than I will happen, so dancing with Delia leading will be good practice.

David was gone for most of the day. I think he was attending one of those dreadful cockfights. I don't understand why someone would want to watch two poor chickens attack each other to death. There are many things about men that puzzle me. I still think of Mr Huntingdon and look forward to his attendance at the assembly. I know I will simply be devastated if he does not return in time.

Tomorrow, we go into Newbury for a Concert. I am greatly looking forward to it

27 May, 1820

Saturday

David and I went riding again. He agreed to an excursion to the village. He had a few shillings on him, which he willingly lent me as I saw some new ribbon of the most dazzling shade of Pomona green. I owe him 2 shillings for the ribbons and 2 farthings to the village boys who I gave them to. They were so very thin and ragged, I felt the need to offer them something to gain sustenance.

Misty was found in Delia's room where she had chewed quite three pairs of shoes. Mother has banned the poor pup to the kennels, but by the gleam in David's eye, I expect her to be returned to the household before a se'nnight is up.

The butcher delivered, with our order, the mail. I had a letter from my cousin, Lady Felicia Osbourne-Browne. She is quite my favourite cousin of my mother's family. She sends me news of her Engagement. He is a fine young man, she writes, of the best family. He is the younger son of Lord Roxburghe. I am unsurprised that Mr Charles Mablethorpe would be her choice; she has long made him the sun around which her written word revolved. He was a soldier during the Peninsular Campaign, and very much the heroic figure. He was seriously injured three times during his years there and at the final battle against the Tyrant at Waterloo. The great Duke of Wellington himself took the young man under his wing during his career and has continued to sponsor him in his budding political career. With the Duke and his Lord Roxburghe's influence, he will be up for a position in the House of Commons in a year or two. I think Felicia will make a delightful society hostess. She is the most graceful and elegant being I have ever met, excepting Mother, of course.

Felicia says she will be married by the end of June. They intend to remain in London until after the King's Coronation. I am hoping they will perhaps be able to stay with us during the journey to their new home.

I sat and wrote her immediately. The groom took my letter, with father's, into the village to be posted.

Dinner was spring Chickens boiled, and a Tongue, a Knuckle of Veal and a fine plum Pudding. Asparagus and green Apricot Tarts.

28 May, 1820

Sunday

We had visitors to our hamlet church today. As we later found out, they were Vicar Wynchester's new students he is tutoring, and their families.

The first was Henry Hylton, son of Sir Paul Hylton, who just recently was given the honour of a Baronetcy for his services to the King. He is a fine doctor, the Vicar said, praising him quite lavishly. His son, Henry (Harry) who is David's age, will be taking intensive tutoring to prepare for his exams. I understand that he will also pursue medicine as his occupation. A very serious expression he wears on his face, but I know I saw a twinkle in his eyes at different comments spoken by the various guests. His older brother Ralph flirted with me with rakish abandon, but my thoughts were only for Mr Huntingdon and not this callow youth.

The other student was a boy younger than myself, no more than 15, I think. He was violently spotted and stuttered when he spoke, Adam Buckman-Smythe. His father is a Colonel of a line regiment and of the Somerset Buckman-Smythes.

After church, we were invited into the Vicarage to have tea

with the two families before they left their sons behind. David and Harry, as he insisted on being called, already seem fast friends.

Molly had a toothache and was indisposed for the day. Sally was required to substitute for her and was saucy to me. I was extremely put out and would have spoken to mother, but David begged me to ignore her manner, for she is suffering the pains of love forsaken. He made me feel quite cruel in forcing him to abandon her, but I know it is best for him.

Delia has started her menses and was quite horrified by the process. Miss Horace was quite red of face as she explained to Delia what was required of her. Delia refused to leave her room for the rest of the day, having her dinner in her room. Poor girl. It is a shock when it happens for the first time. I snuck into her room and gave her some jellied fruits as a treat.

29 May, 1820

Monday

Nothing of significance to report. Delia a little recovered. Not so hysterical. Silly girl.

I visited Misty at the kennels, but rain forced me indoors. I played cards with David and did some embroidery with mother who complimented me on my fine needlework.

Later, as thunder sounded outside the windows, I began re-trimming my bonnet.

30 May, 1820

Tuesday

Sammy is home. He is quite three inches taller and so very gangly. He came in the Sherbourne's carriage. They are [quite] a merry family and will be staying with us until Thursday. Mr and Mrs Sherbourne were all politeness and graciousness. Sammy's friend Freddy Sherbourne is very much the wild boy but charming all the same. His (Freddy's) sister Clementina is my own age and is as excited as I am about being released from the schoolroom. Their middle brother Douglas is on his way to join his regiment. He has newly purchased an ensigncy. While their older sister Philippa is engaged to a young man who works in the East India Company and will be wed next month. And lastly, is the oldest son. Mr Francis Sherbourne. A most amazing man. Most handsome with Mahogany-coloured hair and dark green eyes the colour of warm emeralds. He was most charming and polite.

Young Freddy will be staying with us until Philippa's wedding. Tomorrow we will be having a picnic by the river. I am looking forward to it, for the weather bids to be very fine.

Clementina thinks Misty is utterly adorable and envies us

having the puppy inside. Her mother does not allow animals in the house. My mother was the same, but David gets his way as usual.

David flirted with Clementina throughout dinner. He seems quite taken with her pretty blonde looks. She has the same green eyes as her brother, Francis. She blushed quite frequently during the meal. Dinner had three extra courses to night, for the gratification of our guests. Dessert consisted of Raspberry Puffs, Lemon Tarts, Ratifee-cakes. All so very delicious, I was quite full.

David and I played a duet after dinner and then Clementina sang while I played a couple of the latest airs. Mrs Sherbourne praised my skill highly to my pleasure.

31 May, 1820

Wednesday

I cannot begin to capture the delight that was our picnic. We rode out in the early afternoon, and it seemed the sun shone for our pleasure alone. Douglas Sherbourne rode my Nutmeg, while David selfishly kept Coriander for himself. Papa allowed Mr Sherbourne to have fine hands, as he drove Clementina and I to the river. Mother, Father, the Sherbournes, and Philippa rode in the well-appointed carriage of theirs, while Miss Horace rode with Freddy and Sammy and a seriously displeased Delia in our landau. I think she felt quite left out riding with the two boys, having no girl her own age to keep her company.

Mr Francis Sherbourne was all that was gracious and kind. He spoke most knowledgeably of many subjects. He informed me (and Clementina who looked disinterested by the topic) of the status of the King's government as he works to arrange things more to his liking. Mr Sherbourne complimented me on the fineness of Nutmeg's conformation. I was able to tell him, with pride, that I had the choosing of her.

We arrived at the River, much too soon it seemed. For I nearly had him convinced to allow me to take the reins. He assured me, if it had been his vehicle, he would have gladly allowed me the privilege, but he was hesitant to do what Father might frown upon. The footmen laid out the blankets and food and while the young people walked along the river. David and Douglas were sent, by Clementina, to harvest flowers for her as she and Delia made garlands for us all. Mr Francis Sherbourne and I continued our discussion began on the drive over. He listened to my opinions with decided interest. I was delighted by his extensive knowledge. We found ourselves to have many similar tastes in literature and art. The boys ended up wet and muddy.

Too soon it was time to eat. We circled back to the tree-shaded blankets and ate heartily of the cold collation prepared for us. It was a very merry luncheon, not a cross word was spoken. We played word games and at some point, David was encouraged to confiscate Miss Horace's sketchpad. He has the most amusing way with drawing people. I think sometimes he could rival Cruikshank. It is not all he does, in oil he has quite a way with landscapes. He has something of Turner's dreamy quality in these. But today all the young ones left with a sketch to both amuse and horrify. Clementina almost looked as if she would cry at first until he took it back and sketched some more. Then she smiled. Mr Francis Sherbourne was quite amused by his and thanked David most sincerely. I do like a gentleman to be able to laugh at himself. One does not want to always be serious.

We returned late in the afternoon when the wind began to pick up. With father's permission, Mr Sherbourne allowed me to take the reins. He assured me I was a most accomplished whipster, which left me in blushes. Dinner was a quieter affair than the picnic as the children were in the nursery. Mr Sherbourne took me in to dinner. We had Roast Lamb, a Fat Goose, Boiled Chicken, Lobster, Asparagus, Gooseberry Tarts, and Custards. After dinner, for dessert, we had a Melon, oranges (which Mr Sherbourne peeled for me), Almonds and Raisins.

We played Quadrille after dinner, and I won 0.3.1. It was very pleasant to be the winner, even if I was at David's expense who lost four shillings total.

Miss Horace played a few airs while we had an impromptu dance. Even Mama and Papa joined in. I danced with all the men, and Mr Francis Sherbourne twice. He is very good, even better than David, much better than the dreadful Mr LaRue.

Ah, I am so very tired and cannot wait until morning. Good-night sweet diary.

1 June, 1820

Thursday

The first part of the day was quiet compared to the activity of the picnic the day before. At breakfast, Mr Francis Sherbourne requested the honour of the first dance, and I accepted with the sincerest pleasure.

Soon it was time to prepare for the Assembly. I went up to my room where Molly was waiting. I dressed with all the eagerness that could fill my heart without exploding. Delia came to watch as I donned my exquisite green dress. Powers dressed my hair into the most amazing arrangement, I feared it would fall if I so much as moved, but she assured me not a hair would stray during the evening. Delia admired my shoes, which arrived yesterday. They are from the most expensive shoemaker in London and of the finest quality.

The pearl garland Mama made, necklace and earrings were the perfect affectation to my dress. Papa gave me quite the loveliest fan, ivory sticks with gold tracery on the leaves. It was the most beautiful fan I have ever seen. Papa, after stating I looked a veritable angel, also asked me for a dance and I was delighted to oblige for

Mama has always said he is the most accomplished dancer she has ever known. More of that later when I arrive at that point. Finally, after the longest time I have ever taken to dress, Molly was draping my shawl over my shoulders. It was so warm that evening, I saw no reason for more.

I walked down the stairs and was greeted by several men and Clementina standing impatiently at the bottom of the stairs. David and Douglas Sherbourne's jaws drop which I did not consider to be flattering, for must they not have been amazed to see me look so pretty for such a strong reaction. Mr Francis Sherbourne stepped forward and offered the most engaging smile. He held out his arm, and I felt the most amazing tingle through my fingers as I touched his superfine sleeve. I stood there waiting for Mama and Mrs Sherbourne who joined us before the quarter hour passed. Mr Sherbourne made conversation with me as we waited, only remembering to include Clementina, his brother, and mine, when I turned to them.

We soon arrived at the Assembly rooms, and I did look about for the Promised presence of Mr Huntingdon but was disappointed when I saw he was not there. I had pledged him a dance and now saw I would have to find other partners than his pleasant company. I said my greetings to the Herrons, the Buckminsters and the Wynchesters.

It was whispered that the Countess and her family might attend. I did not believe such rumours because they never appear to prove true. I have seen her in the village once or twice, a very awesome presence. Everything she owns has the proof of Quality about them. Her carriage is of the most luxurious and her clothes of the finest cloth. Her son, Lord Bellewicke married when I was young, but I remember thinking him very handsome even then.

The dancing began and Mr Sherbourne escorted me to the Dance floor where Several couples were already aligned. Robert Herron showed excellent taste in choosing Clementina for the first set. Mr Gregory Herron was partnered with his fiancée. Mr Buckminster was standing beside his wife, Lady Catherine who was dressed in the first stare of elegance. Their daughter Nichola is Delia's age and quite her dearest friend.

Mr Sherbourne was a very fine dancer, but we were able to make little conversation as the dance parted us frequently. However, before the set was over, he had asked for a second to my distinct pleasure. I was dancing with Papa, who proved himself to be the finest dancer I had ever taken the floor with...until later. But not to get before myself.

Just as the music ended, there came late arrivals. It was the Lady Peasedale herself. She is one of the few women in our Great Kingdom to possess a title in her own right. The County of Peasedale being an old and honourable Title. The entire company stood in awe as she made her way into the hall. She wore a most regal costume with a stunning parure of diamonds. As she came further in the room, Lord Bellewicke followed with his wife upon his arm. It is quite unusual to see them in our humble neighbourhood as they generally reside in Staffordshire when not in London.

The Silence which had held the room, dispersed into a hive of conversation once Mr Buckminister stepped forward to welcome them. The Musicians sawed along ignored for several minutes before stopping. The D'Aubigny's made their way around the room with the utmost graciousness greeting the known and making the acquaintance of the unknown. Mama presented me to her Ladyship, and I remember barely breathing as I made my curtsey trying to keep my back properly straight and my knees from failing me. The Countess' hair, the same Ebony as her son, was streaked with Pure white but dressed in an elegant fashion that did not detract from her fine looks.

I was also presented to Lord and Lady Bellewicke. Lady Bellewicke is, there can be no doubt, the loveliest woman ever seen. She was no taller than I, but her hair was the same colour as the silk on Indian Maize. It seemed to gather the candlelight and shine with its own light. She was elegantly slender, no sign of the children she was mother to. Finally, they had been made known to all and the musicians sensibly began to play again. Papa had the pleasure of escorting Lady Peasedale to the floor and Lord Bellewicke insisted on partnering his wife for the first dance. Robert Herron escorted me to the floor, and we stood across from Lord and Lady Bellewicke.

It was a revelation to see a couple, so long married, so very much in love. I saw Lord Bellewicke look down at his wife with near worship in his eyes. I knew in that moment I could never marry for less. Mr Oakley, who is a widower, asked me to dance for the next set. He is quite old and not quite the thing, but it would have appeared ill mannered to refuse his request. He was not a particularly fine dancer, and I spent most of my time trying to keep him with the music rather than ahead of it. We nearly collided with Mr Sherbourne and Lady Bellewicke who gave every appearance of having a delightful time. I was more than relieved when Mr Oakley's set was complete, and I was able to return to Mama's side.

It was with every expectation of having Mr Sherbourne as my partner next and I believe he thought so too for he was making his way to my side when suddenly I found, to my astounded gaze, Mr Huntingdon standing before me. Sometime during my endless set with Mr Oakley, he had arrived and confirmed his permission with Mama for the next dance. Mr Sherbourne arrived at my side just as Mr Huntingdon was holding out his arm. For a moment I was reminded of two hunting spaniels glaring down the other for the right to carry the fallen bird back to their master.

Finally, the silence between them was ended by a word from Mama who invited Mr Sherbourne to sit beside her and Mr Huntingdon escorted me to the forming set. The musician struck up a waltz and Mr Huntingdon took me in his arms to step into the flow of the dancers. It was like floating on air. I have not had any comparable experience to it in my entire life. I never wanted it to end. Mr Huntingdon apologised for his tardy appearance but explained that one of his job horses threw a shoe on the last stage and he nearly feared not making it. He rode the lead horse to town and with his formal attire in his saddlebag and sent a groom from the inn back for his curricle and man.

He was there, and every bit as delightful as I remembered him to be. His azure eyes gazed at me with such admiration that I was frequently covered in blushes.

Mr Sherbourne was at my side as soon as we were off the dance floor and looked with annoyance at Mr Huntingdon as introductions were performed on their behalf. Mr Sherbourne escorted me around the room as the musicians took a short break, I felt Mr Huntingdon's eyes follow us but was much engrossed in Mr Sherbourne's words. He expressed himself most earnestly to require me to save the next waltz for him. Emboldened by his blatant interest, I assured him the next waltz would be his. I was most anxious to experience that magical delight again, and with him.

The evening seemed to continue as a dream. I danced with Lord Bellewicke, and I spoke to Lady Bellewicke after, she was kindness itself and complimented me on both my appearance and poise.

Harry Hylton shyly required a dance of me before Douglas Sherbourne insisted on dancing with me. It was quite the rompish dance for he has none of his brother's elegant skill but rather a boyish enthusiasm. David insisted on the next and then it was the Waltz with Mr Sherbourne. Oh, my mind cannot decide who was the better dancer. Both moved with grace, but their styles were inexpressibly different.

I danced all the remaining dances, and the final one with Mr Huntingdon. I can still hear the music the fiddlers played. I am unsure if I sway, as I am writing, to the memory of the music or from utter exhaustion.

I best sleep for the sun is sneaking through my windows and I do not want to sleep the day away as the Sherbournes will be leaving in the afternoon. I am delirious with exhaustion, but it is such a happy sort.

Tomorrow holds such promise but yet sadness too. I cannot wait to see what it brings.

2 June, 1820

Friday

It was striking the noon hour when I made my way downstairs. I found I was before most of my fellow residents. There were none in the parlour, but I heard sounds from my father's study and peeked in. Papa waved me in, bless him! Mr Francis Sherbourne was in enjoying a coze with him. Papa smiled most benignly upon me and suggested I show Mr Sherbourne the gardens, for surely on such a beautiful day he would prefer to spend his remaining hours before their departure out of doors.

Mr Sherbourne and I walked through the gardens. The gardeners were out in force and seemed to be around every corner. Mr Sherbourne, Francis, and I talked about everything it seemed. He told me his plans for the future, we talked about what we liked to read, what was our favourite songs were. No topic seemed off limits. Too soon it seemed David, Douglas, and Clementina found us, and we were dragged back into the dreary indoors to say our farewells.

Clementina and I have promised to write each other. David will be writing Douglas. I feel assured to hear news of Mr Sherbourne and hope we will meet again, for he is one of the most pleasant men of my acquaintance.

We had barely seen the Sherbournes off when a curricle came up the drive. Mr Cole Huntingdon had come to pay his respects. He came in and spoke to us for the polite length of time and just before he was to leave, he begged permission to take me for a drive. I was only too eager to agree.

Mr Huntingdon let me drive. His fine pair were spirited beasts, and it took nearly all my attention to control them, but he never made to take them over. His faith in my ability was exceedingly satisfying. I cannot but feel complimented by his attentions to me. He drove on the return, and we were able to talk though with circumspection as his groom hanging on the back could hear our every word.

The day was quiet after. I suddenly was so very tired and with mother's permission returned upstairs to nap. I woke in time for dinner, and we had a pleasant family meal. Tomorrow we are to dine at the Vicar's, and Mr Huntingdon will be there.

3 June, 1820

Saturday

David woke with a fever, so fearfully hot it was. Mama sent for the doctor. He came and bled David; left packets of dreadful looking powders and promised to return on the morrow to check for improvement.

The day progressed and though I wished to help tend him, Mama banished me from the sickroom not wishing for me to become ill as well. I was restless and a part of me selfish. For if David was too sick, we would not be attending the Vicar's dinner tonight. I tried to sew, I tried to read, I tried to practise, nothing kept my mind settled.

Mother took me aside around two and told me she was severely disappointed in my conduct. She felt that if one ball and the attentions of a few handsome gentlemen were so turning my head, she was prepared to send me back to the schoolroom. I felt she was being unjust since she would not allow me to assist in David's recovery. I submitted to Mother's lecture in silence until the end and then chose to defend myself. She had banished me from David's room, and left me without a purpose for the day, to balance against my concern. How could I focus on trivialities when all my worries were centred upon him? Mother gave me a shrewd look that told me that it was most likely she was able to discern my secret worry as well as my obvious one, but I met her eyes with as clear a conscience as I could for a girl who longed to be tending her brother with an equal desire to attend the Vicar's dinner.

David was very little better at tea time, Mother sent a message to the Vicarage explaining we would be absent. I am sad not to go but even sadder that David is not sufficiently better.

Finally, I was able to persuade Mother that my need to tend a beloved suffering brother outweighed the risks of exposure to the illness. I was able to mop his brow and spoon feed him water gruel. Mama was pleased by his improvement before sending me off to bed.

She believes his fever to have broken. Thank God! I intend to wake early so I may visit him before the doctor comes to check upon him. I have little doubt he will cup David again, not something I enjoy watching.

4 June, 1820

Sunday

David was worse in the morning, Mother quite concerned. Miss Horace took Delia and Sammy to church, Mama allowed me to stay with her and David. I did not want to leave him and only did so when the doctor cupped him. After the doctor left, I was allowed to return to the sickroom. I could not bear to leave him; he was so flushed along his cheekbones but other than that looked so very pale. Poor David! I read to him for hours while he drifted between sleep and waking. Each time he returned from slumber, he would look at me with that infinitely gratifying smile and my heart would just melt. I cannot but be concerned for him. He is rarely ill, but when he has become so, he has come close to death each time. There was the Scarlet Fever when he was eight and the fall from his horse when he was twelve and broke his collar bone. Where this fever came from, I do not know, but since he is the only one to show signs, I would hazard that horrid cockfight to be the source of exposure.

I had time during the long hours of sleep to think of Mr Huntingdon and wonder if he had missed me last night. Vicar Wynchester sent sincere and anxious enquiries after David's health and fruit was sent over from his garden for David when he is feeling more the thing.

When I left, David was sleeping peacefully, and Mother is confident he will be much improved by morning. I sleep now so I may wake early to see if her apparently sanguine expectations prove true.

5 June 1820

Monday

David is so much better today. The convalescent was allowed to sit up after the Doctor's visit and was not even cupped today because the Doctor felt he was so much better. I read to him again during the morning, but by time for nuncheon Mama felt he was well enough to send me out for a walk in the garden as she worried I might become ill tending him.

Walking through the garden, reminded me of one so recently taken in Mr Sherbourne's company. It was nearly prescient my thinking of him, for with the mails came a letter from Clementina who gave me details of the family. Douglas looks elegant in his new uniform she says. Mr Francis Sherbourne spends little time at home as he is a member of Whites and also has many sporting friends who careen in and out of the Sherbourne's London establishment. She has attended a few smaller parties, as she is not officially out. She begs me most hastily to respond and offers to send me the latest fashion plates if I so desire. Could this be in doubt?

Tomorrow David will be allowed out of bed, if he continues to show improvement. I hope for it more than anything.

6 June 1820

Tuesday

David is so entirely improved I was able to accept to Mr Huntingdon's invitation to drive with an easy heart. David teased me most mercilessly about my suitor and I could do little but blush in response. I do like Mr Huntingdon very well. David also teased me for fickleness, for he saw I found Mr Sherbourne wholly attractive. It is true, I did and do. I wonder if it is possible to be in love with two men at once?

Mr Huntingdon again let me drive; we stopped for Tea at the Vicarage. Mr Harry Hylton and young Adam joined us. Mrs Wynchester was very kind in her concerns for David. She sent along her rhubarb concoction for him.

Mr Huntingdon informed me, with true reluctance, he would be leaving our pleasant hamlet on Thursday. I am very sorry to see him leave and can but regret that as soon as I meet an amiable man he departs.

Dinner today was Roast Chicken and Knuckle of Veal. We had the first Strawberries of the season, sweet plump berries. I took up a bowl with some fresh cream for David who had been sent back to bed after overexerting himself during the day. He was pleased with my offering and asked me to stay to play chess. I was willing to provide him any entertainment, which might make his confinement more pleasant. I won the first and last games, David the middle.

7 June, 1820

Wednesday

In apology for our lack of appearance to the Wynchester's dinner, Mama held a dinner party for the Wynchesters today. It was something last minute, but David was well enough to attend which was all that mattered to us.

Naturally the Wynchesters' guest and older pupil were invited. At the last minute, we were notified of an extra guest. The Vicar's younger son was passing through on his way to his new living which is situated on the border of Cornwall.

Brian seemed destined for the church from an early age, I remember his sermons to us younger children well from our time spent in his presence. Fortunately, the passing of years has tempered his manner, so he no longer gives offence with every word which parts from his mouth.

I was escorted to dinner by Mr Huntingdon with Brian on my other side. To even the number of men to women, Miss Horace was invited to dinner. She sat between Mr Wynchester on the one side and Brian on the other.

It was a very pleasant evening.

We played Quadrille after dinner, and I won 2 shillings 3 farthings.

Mr Huntingdon leaves early tomorrow. I know I shall miss him as I hope he will miss me. He assures me he will be back, by the latest in Autumn. How far away that seems now.

It was cloudy today, but no rain fell until fifteen minutes ago.

8 June, 1820

Thursday

Everything was quiet today, David was from bed during the day, but very passive in his manner. His recovery is assured, but slower than Mama wishes. I see her watching him with concern when she thinks no one is looking.

Sally brought herself to my attention again. She was tending a fire when she ran from the room suddenly. When Molly came to complete her tasks, I enquired to Sally's location. She explained that Sally had come down ill and Mrs Girling had assigned Molly to take her duties for the day.

I took a tour of the Nursery and saw Delia downhearted and Sammy restless. The light rain of yesterday, had become a downpour today. I convinced Delia and Sammy to join me in the Attic. There has been the suggestion of a Masquerade ball at the Assembly Hall in another month and Mama gave permission to check the trunks for old dresses. Sammy was allowed to run wild as he chose in the other part and get as dusty as he pleased which left him contented and tired after Delia and I were finished checking every trunk.

I found Mama's court dress, a very elaborate arrangement and hoop skirt. The style is not what I choose to wear, but the hoop and the fabric will be the basis for my costume. Mother has suggested I make the costume myself though she has promised Powers' assistance. I think this project is mother's way of keeping me busy as I believe she still feels my head to have been turned by the sudden spate of socialising our tiny hamlet has been privileged to hold.

Dinner was a Roast Beef and Shank of Ham. We had fresh Peas and Asparagus. Raspberry Tarts and Lemon Puffs. I ate too many tarts, and David teased me as he is wont to do.

I know I will need to do something active to compensate as my dresses feel a mite too tight, but Molly tells me that where it is tight is not from too much food but too much growth. She says I have a fine figure and should be proud of it. I do not know how I feel about this.

9 June, 1820

Friday

Harry Hylton has asked to call on us tomorrow as he has no lessons on Saturday. He has use of a horse, so the three of us will go riding.

Mother has decided I have been ignoring my accomplishments and has set me a schedule of practice. I HAD thought I was done with the schoolroom!

In the morning, I practised the Piano for an hour, then I practised singing while Delia played, she plays poorly for her age. She has not practised at all faithfully and it shows in her stumbling performance. My singing must improve by default for I must pay more attention to the correct note to be sung as I can put no dependence upon the one being played.

After nuncheon, David sat with me, and we drew together. He has such natural ability, I hope to improve under his tutelage.

After drawing we went for a ride, Nutmeg, and Coriander were happy to see us after so much rain. The paths were muddy, and poor Nutmeg was covered and so was the hem of my riding costume. My hat was knocked askew from a branch that was half broken.

On our return, mother put me to work sewing. I was set to help Miss Horace repair Delia and Sammy's mending. Not a task I particularly enjoy. By dinner, I was nearly ready to go to bed, I hadn't a moment to myself and in my room, I might sneak in the next chapter of the lovely, scandalous (or so Mama would think) novel. I will not put the title in this diary.

Finally, after a long dinner, Mother gave me permission to retire to my room, where I am writing this and then on to my novel.

10 June, 1820

Saturday

Today was nearly a copy of yesterday but for the riding with Harry. He is a very nice boy, though very shy. I think Mr Wynchester convinced him to write his note yesterday, for though I see his desire for company, he put himself forward not at all and did not speak unless spoken too.

David and I have invited him to ride with us whenever he has time from his lessons and the weather is willing. His face showed such a light of happiness at our suggestion. I think his is an acquaintance we will be able to cherish, I can only hope he will find our friendship equally as valuable.

Ate little dinner tonight, my throat coming on putrid before dinner was served and worse when food was subjected to it. Mother sent me to bed early with a flannel wrap for my throat.

She does not know I got back up to write this and would be upset if she did.

11 June 1820

Sunday

Mama decided I was too ill to go to Church with the family. She set Molly to watch me when they went. I convinced Molly to read my book to me. She read very haltingly, but I helped her with the bigger words.

Mother had the doctor look at me. He wanted to cup me, something I dislike very much. It makes me quite faint to see my own blood. Mama gave in to me. If my fever does not come down by tomorrow though, I will be cupped.

I pretended to be asleep to write this. I think my fever has gone down, but I am not sure.

13 June 1820

Tuesday

My fever became much worse. Mama had me cupped and spent nearly the whole of Monday in my room. There was no opportunity for me to write. I did nothing but sleep restlessly and have my brow wiped with lavender water. I was spoon fed barley water and milk gruel at infrequent intervals—neither to my taste.

Better today, but still weak. I feel awful and wish to be allowed up to wash at the basin. David was allowed in to see me. He read to me for a while and when mother and Molly left the room, told me funny stories which Mama would surely frown upon.

I was allowed soup for dinner and some chicken. It is a large improvement upon gruel.

I hope to get up tomorrow.

14 June 1820

Wednesday

Feeling better has a side less pleasing, as Mother insisted I return to my studies. To make sure I stayed rested, I practised French and German with Miss Horace.

Later Mama had me audit her accounts as an exercise in arithmetic and household concerns. She has decided I will also plan the menus for the following week and assess the state of the kitchen. I to go against the will of Cook? I do not have such bravery in me. She is a formidable creature very large and ill-tempered. The maids all fear her wooden spoons and the courageous ones have made complaints to Mrs Girling. But Cook has been with us since before David's birth and nothing short of murder would dislodge her.

Tomorrow, Mother has agreed I may ride Nutmeg if I continue improving. David rode her for me today so she would not feel neglected. I ate a fine dinner of Roast Beef, and the fresh Fish David caught in the stream that runs behind the house.

Sammy read this evening before he was sent up to bed. Mother is very pleased with his progress. He expresses himself with fine emotion as he recounts the story. Unlike Delia who has not learned this particular art, he makes the story come alive. We hear the humour, the joy, the pathos. He would have made a fine actor if he had been born to a different station in life.

Earlier Misty crept into my room and is sleeping on my bed, legs kicking at the air as if she is chasing a rabbit. Do dogs dream?

15 June, 1820

Thursday

I received my second letter from Clementina, my emotions are quite agitated by her words. My jealousy is overwhelming and quite wrong I know Mama would say. She is attending so many exciting parties in London. She writes about the preparations for Philippa's wedding which is soon to happen. Also, Mr Francis Sherbourne has distinguished her new friend Miss Warwicke with his attentions. Sophia, as Clementina already calls her is, I'm told, a most handsome girl. I am sorrowed to think myself forgotten already.

Mr Harry Hylton joined David and I on our ride today. He is very sweet to me when he forgets to stare at his boots and blush. We met with Robert Herron while riding along the border of his property. He flirted with me, something he does with every girl he meets. He and David fell behind Harry and I and talked for several minutes.

After Dinner, David excused himself for the evening. Under Mother's questioning he admitted to meeting Mr Herron but would say no more. I am sure he is planning on attending a cock-fight or something equally barbaric.

Misty again on my bed, Molly complains about the hairs she leaves behind, but I see her sneaking in a pat here and there.

16 June, 1820

Friday

David came to breakfast with a swollen eye and bruised chin, mother was horrified but he would admit nothing of what happened. Later, after much persuasion, he admitted to me he had attended a cockfight. Having laid a wager on the red-combed cock he was very angry when the loser refused to make payment. He and Robert took on this dishonourable creature and his brutish companion in a bruising fight which left both marked.

Mother is most seriously displeased with Mr Herron, and has indicated to David he is not welcome, at present, in our home. Naturally she believes Mr Herron to have led David astray, I sometimes think she does not know her son well. He is nearly always spoiling for an adventure, and it is as likely that David told Robert of the event as the opposite.

Papa has said very little on the subject, at least not in my hearing.

I am back to my daily routine. Piano practice, watercolours, mending.

After nuncheon I spent a very long time in the kitchen with Cook, where she acquainted me with the elements that make up her world. I watched as she ordered the kitchen maids and scullery maid around like serfs. I am sure I saw the scullery maid cry. She is easily but two years older than Delia. Such a young girl to work so hard.

After my time with Cook, Mr Owens, the Butler, showed me the pantry, and Mrs Girling, the Housekeeper, introduced me to the stores of spices kept under lock and key. Dinner came soon upon the heels of the Housekeeper returning me to the front rooms.

I ate while Mother asked me questions about the food, making me think about the taste and preparation rather than just liking it or not liking it. After father went to his study taking David with him, Mother told me how important it is for a wife to attend to the household. To make sure the meals are varied, the food of good quality and not just acceptable. That a husband may not know why he is dissatisfied with his dinner, but that a wife must know why so as to correct the cook. Mama says I will, over the next three weeks, begin taking over all her duties until I can run the household for a month on my own. She assures me I have learned or will learn all the knowledge I need to know this way. Not only will I be giving orders to Cook for dinner, but Mrs Girling and Mr Owens. Our butler has always seemed to look down his very long nose at me as if I was a smelly, dirty child. If I ever dare to command his attention and actions, will he listen?

17 June, 1820

Saturday

Mama gave me the day off from my training. David and I took Delia and Sammy out for a morning of fishing. Sammy was ill-humoured and finally we sent him home with the groom. I felt extreme remorse when we returned and found out he has a toothache, has since Thursday but had said nothing.

Mama is unhappy with the state of his tooth, she has examined it, and it looks quite bad. She says if it does not improve, we may be making a trip to London. She only trusts the tooth-drawer who extracted two teeth from Papa last year.

Dinner was fine, Papa complimented me on my choices. David asked why I did not choose more sweets.

Sammy no better at end of day.

18 June, 1820

Sunday

Prayers were said to honour the dead of Waterloo on this fifth anniversary of that glorious defeat of the Tyrant Napolean and the ghastly loss of English men. Today's sermon was on the parable of the talents. Mr Wynchester explained the importance of using what God endowed us with for His glory. He told us, each of us, we must look inside and find what abilities God granted us and use them, develop them for the greater good. He chastised unnamed Parish members with a hard stare telling them God would be disappointed with the neglected talents they had been given.

At one point I feared he was looking at me, but I think there must have been someone behind me for he spoke to me most kindly after the service. Harry Hylton was there and seemed happy to have a chance to speak to both David and I. Adam Buckman-Smythe looked uncomfortable every time Mr Wynchester's gaze fell upon him. It was only then I remembered Adam had been sitting two seats behind me.

Upon returning home, mother decided I should read to the servants from the Bible. I did as she asked picking the Parable of the Prodigal Son for my passage.

Sammy is no better and Mother fears his jaw has swollen too. Papa is arranging the stages for our trip to London. Mother has decided we should all go, and Mr Spelling will examine all our Teeth. I remember last time we went; he filed two of my back teeth and threatened to pull one if I did not tend my teeth better.

David has convinced our Parents to stay home, letting Mother examine the state of his teeth in his bid to remain. He winked to me afterwards, a sure indication of mischief on his part.

Delia is nearly as excited as I at the idea of visiting the Metropolis. Neither of us are looking forward to visiting Mr Spelling and his den of horrors, but Mama has promised we may visit the Menagerie, shop at the warehouses and I will be allowed to buy one dress by one of the select Modistes in town.

I am very excited and though I wish no suffering upon Sammy, cannot be but delighted at the opportunity his injury will provide.

Dinner was badly chosen today, I did not realise how badly certain dishes go together. I will do better tomorrow.

19 June, 1820

Monday

We left early in the day, Molly sat between Delia and I. Mother across from me, Sammy by her and Powers across from Delia. It is fortunate we are all slender women, or we would have been entirely more discomforted than we were. Papa was fortunate in riding alongside. Our coachman is a very good driver which is lucky as a stage coach, at one point, careened past us with all the reckless disregard of a whirlwind. We have a cart following with the valet and our baggage.

It was a very long day, and I am nearly too tired to write this. I did little, but the enforced confinement is more wearying than anything. And poor Sammy, how he suffers. Mother gave him several drops of laudanum and he slept most of the way, but still he moaned and was restless the whole trip.

We changed horses in Reading at the local coaching inn, they were amazingly fast in changing the horses. I had barely time to catch my breath, and we were on our way again.

At Maidenhead we stopped for nuncheon. I was greatly relieved to stretch my legs and stop swaying for a too brief hour. I was not motion sick, but Delia felt it terribly. Molly was nearly green from it. But this is her first trip from the village and will learn to adjust to it. She rode with the Valet on the second half of the trip. The cart was going at a slower pace. Powers moved to our side with Delia in the middle and poor moaning Sammy lying on the seat with his head on Mother's lap.

Our last stop before London was in Hounslow and they changed our horses in less than a minute. Papa timed them with his watch. We arrived through Cumberland Gate at Grillon's Hotel. Mother prefers it to the Pulteney where the Russian Emperor stayed back during the peace of 1814. She felt he and his sister were rude to our then Prince Regent. Mother will admit our Gracious King has not always acted as he should (though only reluctantly) but it was England that made Europe safe from that horrid beast Bonaparte. Oh my, I have listened to that discussion too many times from Mama.

Delia and I are sharing a room; Molly has a cot with us. Mama dosed Sammy with laudanum, sent a groom off to deliver a message to the tooth-drawer and we went down to dinner. We are all quite tired from our journey, so mother sent us to bed early. Neither Delia nor I are looking forward to having our teeth examined tomorrow. I do not wish my teeth prodded, poked or filed again. Horrid!

20 June, 1820

Tuesday

My teeth are in excellent condition I am told. Mr Spelling suggested filing one tooth, but when I was reluctant and looked to Mother, he withdrew his suggestion. Sammy had his bad tooth pulled and Delia two filed. After that the day got much better.

We went shopping. First to the warehouse. Mama gave me several guineas to spend as I wished. I did. A fan, a parasol, some stockings. We bought several ells of fabric and as a grand treat Mama took me to La Robe de la Reine. Everyone says it is the most exclusive establishment in society. You may only get an appointment if you have a recommendation from another client. Mama was recommended by her brother's wife, Lady Welbourne.

I was quite nervous as we entered the establishment. It is positively the most elegant shop. The main room resembles a parlour and Madame St. Germaine is a most formidable lady. She looked down this long thin nose at me and I felt entirely unworthy. She is known to be a French Émigré, it is said she is of their nobility. The rumours also say she has a partner who is a Comtesse.

Madame sent me off to a room to have my measurements taken by a pretty spoken French girl only a few years older than myself. Madame and mother stayed in the parlour and took tea while they waited. When I returned, Madame began showing me sketchbooks and let me make a choice of a ball dress. Oh, it is going to be the most beautiful dress ever. A light bluish purple to highlight my eyes and gold and pearls to accent the bodice. Oh, my and the neckline is the most daring I have will have ever worn. Madame promises no dress made by her will ever look like mine. A note will be made which style and colour was created.

I know this dress will be ruinously expensive, but I cannot regret the price to have such a lovely dress. After my dress was chosen, we went calling on friends and family. First to my Uncle's, the Earl of Welbourne, to thank his lady wife for her generosity. She was quite amused by my enthusiasm. My cousin, Edmund came in from riding in the Park while we were there. He enquired most politely after me and offered to take me riding in the Park, if my stay was long enough, offering his younger brother's gelding without a second thought. With a nod from Mama, I said yes for already I miss Nutmeg.

After visiting more family, we finally arrived at the Sherbourne house. Clementina was entirely surprised to see me and could not exclaim enough at my presence. She immediately asked if we would be attending any of the social occasions happening. Mama said yes, we would, she already had (much I knew) several invitations.

My delight is inestimable.

Tonight, Papa got us tickets to the theatre. I did not know where to look first, so many things to see. The stage, the boxes. The pretty ladies and handsome men. Papa pointed out a Duke across from me! (when I asked him to tell me who everyone was). Mama stopped him at this point, so I did not find out who was in the boxes beside him. I think she did not like us talking during the farce. The Duke was not very handsome but instead very old and slept through the performance. Beside him was a pretty girl who must have been his granddaughter. She spent much of the performance flirting with handsome young men. Why was she allowed to wear so many diamonds when I am only allowed Pearls, I do not know. Also, her dress was lower cut then my new one will be. I wonder if I should ask mother if mine should be too if this is the fashion?

It was a wonderful night.

21 June, 1820

Wednesday

I saw Mr Francis Sherbourne today when Clementina and I went for a walk. He remembers me well. I also met Miss Warwicke, I did not think her such a well-favoured girl, her lips were quite thin and her nose very large. I believe she uses rice powder to cover her spots. But Mr Sherbourne must admire her to take her for a drive. She seemed a silly girl, frightened of horses and seemed only to have accepted the drive because Mr Sherbourne agreed not to move the horses above a slow walk.

Clementina is going to a dancing party tomorrow and said she may take a guest. Mama gave her approval with Mrs Sherbourne to chaperone me. I am so very pleased to be able to attend. Mama has already told me we will be staying until Uncle Welbourne's Midsummer's Eve Ball. And she has assured me that Madame St. Germaine will have my dress completed by this time. All the accessories to match the dress were also purchased from La Robe de la Reine and they will be delivered with the dress. Mama never even told me she had Molly bring my pearls. Mother must have known of the ball before we came.

I cannot bear the wait until Friday.

Tonight, we dined *en famille* with Papa's brother, Lord Wandesforde, and his family. Madeleine and her twin Edward (Maddy and Ned) are just 18 and were quite amusing. They seem ready for any sport that may be proposed and have no fear about suggesting their own. It is Madeleine's first season, and she was taken by the Ton with enthusiasm. She has had five proposals she told me when we played a duet on the piano. She has a much prettier singing voice than I, though not as good as Delia's (but more practised).

My cousin, Julian is a very handsome man and ever so kind. He has invited me to ride in the Park, tomorrow. He has the most amazing eyes of brown with coppery flecks. It has been many years since last we met. All I remember about him was a tall lengthy youth who would have nothing to do with his younger siblings, and myself by extension. I can say happily this is no longer true. Though he does still tease Maddy and Ned something terrible. They care nought but beleaguer him in return.

We read poetry to each other. Cousin Julian knows the most beautiful poetry. He has even agreed to let me take the reins of his high-steppers, as he refers to them. So much excitement planned in so little time.

I find I do very much like the city.

22 June, 1820

Thursday

We received my dress today; I had to try it on immediately. It is even more lovely that I could have imagined. When I gave the dress back to Molly, she held up a weed, or so I thought. She explained it was Goldenrod. She stitched it into the hem of my dress and promised me I would see my true love after midnight. Oh, it would be lovely to know who that might be. I have felt my heart flutter at the presence of two men since my removal from the schoolroom. Could one of them be my true love? (but how could it be Mr Sherbourne, he has made his preference for this Miss Warwicke quite clear!)

Cousin Julian and I drove to the park. He let me take the reins for a short time, but I soon gave them back for I could see it made him nervous to not have the leather straps between his very capable fingers.

Mr Francis Sherbourne was there riding with a friend of his, Mr Benedict De Moreville. A man with very pretty eyes, but not a very prepossessing face. It looks as if his nose has been broken quite three times for it seems to change directions that many times on its way down to the tip. But he appears a sensible man anxious to please his companions.

I do believe Mr Sherbourne was less than sanguine to see me driving out with such a blade of fashion as my cousin. I do believe Julian read his displeasure, for he flirted with me quite prominently as we spoke to Mr Sherbourne and Mr de Moreville. I was assured the Sherbourne's would be attending my Uncle's ball, and I learned it was a celebratory ball for my Cousin's recent marriage (did Mama tell me this and I forgot? How silly my memory can be.) Both men requested a dance with me, which I was perfectly happy to grant.

After my drive with Cousin Julian, the day seemed to pass with amazing speed. Mama insisted we have an early night as we would see little sleep the next. I was so excited at the prospect it was so very very hard to get to sleep. Delia was wroth with me for keeping her awake. She is also very jealous to not be able to attend the Midsummer Eve ball. She and Sammy will stay at Acherton House for the night with my poor Sixteen-year-old cousin, who is not out of the schoolroom. She too is out of temper for being too young for the ball.

It is a shame they cannot come and enjoy the celebration, but just as I had to wait to outgrow the schoolroom, so must they.

23 June, 1820

Friday

Dawn is here and truly the 24th but I must tell of the ball on the correct date and eventually I will sleep to bring on the *"new day"*.

Mother wished me to sleep in, but the early night and my heart filled with excitement I could not stay asleep. I can barely keep still. Mother has had me practise my dance steps with Papa one more time for her eagle eye to examine while she played the piano. I did not know she could play so well. I was very proud of her skill.

I remember little of the day. We had a light dinner. Enough to hold us until the Midnight supper. There are many balls tonight, Mama said. So, she said many of our acquaintances would not arrive until later as they will have obligations to stop into others before coming to Lord Welbourne's. I was amused by this statement, the assumption everyone wanted to be at my Uncle's ball in preference to any other. Now I know why. It was [the] most magnificent...

But I get ahead of myself.

After dinner, I changed into the ball dress (mother was not taking chances on stains or wrinkles. As if I'm a child!!!) I looked, yes, I will say it and risk heaven's wrath. I looked pretty. Molly said I looked *"Very pretty."* After Powers dressed my hair and my toilet was complete, and Molly and I were alone, I spun around the room again and again until she had to hold me up from falling. I was as giddy as if I had drunk a bottle of champagne on my own.

We arrived at the ball. I was introduced to Cousin, Lady Felicia's new husband. A fine man who has been in Australia in the Governor's retinue. He was promoted on this last trip home therefore the marriage was moved up and she will be returning with him. She took me aside after the guests were greeted and told me much of the delights she looks forward to. I think perhaps her enthusiasm is much to convince herself for it must be frightening to go to a place so far away and where you will know no one.

The dancing did not start immediately. First, we had time to walk the length of the room, which was already mightily full, and meet new acquaintances and greet old.

The Sherbournes arrived at the ball, soon after us, but Mr Francis Sherbourne was not with them. I was disappointed at first until Clementina told me he would be joining them later with Mr de Moreville in tow. I was pleased for I did not want to dance only with cousins. I do wish David had come, he would have had such a pleasurable time too for he loves dancing nearly as much as I.

Cousin Julian and the rest of the family were there when we arrived. Cousin Julian and I danced the first. Ned and I the second. I was beginning to fear I would only dance with family when a very nice youth asked me to dance. I do not recall his name for it is too late, and I learned too many, but he was very sweet and complimentary. His dancing will need improving, but he did not step on my hem or toes for which I was grateful.

Uncle Wandesforde asked me to dance, he is nearly as good as Papa, though not quite as much. He told me I was lovely, and he had no objection to my taking his son's fancy so strongly. I could not but blush, I did not think Cousin Julian had any particular interest in me.

A few more dances with men who blur in my mind, and it was supper time, Cousin Julian took me to supper. He filled my plate with too much food but simply called a footman to take it when I declared myself too full to eat a bite more. I was sitting, laughing over something silly when I saw Mr Huntingdon. He looked very fine wearing a well-cut dark blue coat to match his azure eyes.

Julian and I had but stood and taken one step from the table and he was standing before me bowing elegantly over my hand and asking me to dance. I assured him of my agreement but explained the next dance was taken. He told me he would be at my side the moment I stepped off the dance floor and then he stepped back to let us pass.

Cousin Julian laughed at my earnest beau however I could not but be complemented by his faithful admiration. Unlike some! As I was circling the room with Cousin Ned, I saw Mr Sherbourne! Dancing with Miss Warwicke. It quite spoiled my humour for the length of the dance, but Mr Huntingdon soon put me to rights. I could not take a step wrong, say a word that was not to his taste. I was a perfect dancer, my appearance dazzled him more than the sun. He was metaphorically at my feet. His words were nigh on poetic.

I was so intoxicated by his admiration; I did not want to be parted from such a fount of approval. It was with reluctance I accepted my next partner. I do not think Mr de Moreville read my distraction. I certainly hope not for he is a perfectly acceptable partner. But his compliments fell flat compared to Mr Huntingdon's.

Mr Sherbourne approached me as we made to the edges of the room. He gracefully reminded me of my promise and though I was still perturbed by his preference for Miss Sophia Warwicke, I agreed and took his proffered arm.

At first, I had nothing to say to him, so only answered his courteous questions, but soon he beguiled me in forgetting my pettishness and we were enjoying our dance and conversation quite well.

Oh, am I so fickle to find so many men attractive? Mr Huntingdon and Mr Sherbourne, and yes *even* Cousin Julian. I did not realise I could feel that frisson until he stood beside me while we watched... Oh goodness I keep getting ahead of myself.

After my dance with Mr Sherbourne and his insistence on the next waltz. I told him it would have to be the one after (for Mr Huntingdon was wise enough to request the forthcoming one.) Mr Sherbourne accepted this but glared at Cousin Julian as he came to claim me. Not for a dance, for he had his limit for the evening. But to escort me outside where everyone was gathering.

Uncle Welbourne shot off Fireworks. They were magnificent, and it was standing beside Cousin Julian, watching his reaction to the sky lit night that I felt such exciting sensations. The touch of his arm under my gloved hand felt for a moment as hot as the flames exploding in the night just as he looked down at me with a look of awe to match my own.

Oh, my head spins. Mama is right. My mind is turned madly by all the excitement. Nothing is sensible about my thoughts.

The first waltz was played once the guests had returned inside. Mr Huntingdon, Cole. He told me my eyes shone more brightly than the fireworks. For the first few steps I was torn between my thoughts of Cousin Julian and my attraction to Cole, but then as he held me a little closer than proscribed, I forgot all but the warm touch of his hand on my back and the other tangled with my fingers, holding me with gentle, but firm strength.

A few more dances passed until the next waltz. Men who blur and fade who cannot stand against the trio who dazzles and tears my heart apart.

And then, Mr Sherbourne, Francis. He held me, even tighter than Mr Huntingdon, I think. His words of praise left me torn, had he said the same to Miss Warwicke? Was I just amusement when she was not there for his attention?

The ball ended just before four and I was glad to sink into the coach and be carried home for my feet were in misery, my slippers in shreds. I had one tear on the hem from a clumsy partner.

Molly was waiting for me, barely awake. I recounted her the evening (though not telling her my accompanying feelings) and she asked if I had seen my True Love, as she unpicked the goldenrod from the hem before hanging it up. I told her I did not know (for how can I know when my feelings are so torn?) She told me to put it under my pillow so I might dream of him. I have never heard this part of the *"spell"* but will gladly do it if it will show me clarity.

24 June, 1820

Saturday

I slept the morning away. Not a surprise I suppose. We had many visitors in our private parlour at Grillon's.

Mr Huntingdon, with his Mother and married sister. They were both very kind to me and I blushed for it must mean his interest is not passing if he takes the time to acquaint me with his family. His mother is invalidish, so she did not attend the ball or, he said when we had a nearly private moment, he would have been very happy to have introduced them last night. He did not explain his sister's absence, but even I could see she was increasing, and a long night of dancing would not be recommended by any attending physician.

Mr Sherbourne, with Clementina. Philippa and Douglas all showed just as the Huntingdons were leaving. They asked if Sammy could spend the day with Freddy. And Mr Sherbourne asked me to go for a drive. Oh my, I have so many invitations and we leave on Monday. I did turn him down, for mother would not approve of it on Sunday. She expects a quiet day after we attend Church (with Mr Huntingdon's family — clever man.)

Cousin Julian with Maddy and Ned came next. We are

attending an evening party with them this evening. Cousin Julian told me I looked as fresh as a newly opened rose, which makes me suspect him of telling Banbury tales for I am quite haggard from the night before.

Afterwards we had a few more people visit, young men who had been a blur the night before were not much clearer today for I was near to falling asleep again I was so tired. Once the last guest left, mother sent me back up to bed to rest for the evening.

I woke up with a headache, Powers gave me a tisane and bless the Lord, but it worked very quickly.

Cousin Julian barely left my side during the evening. He even turned the pages for me as I played a song for the company. I was well received, and I give mother's insistence on my regular practice the credit it deserves. The admiration in Julian's dark eyes as he applauded my talent had quite an emboldening effect on me. I flirted with him, and he seemed pleased with my ingénue attempt.

I went to sleep and dreamt of nothing. I did not recall my dream the night/morning before (For Molly did ask) but I do know I dreamt. Perhaps I will remember it later and finally know where my heart will settle?

25 June, 1820

Sunday

I was sad at first as I sat in the pew, listening to a strange Vicar announce God's meaning. I missed Mr Wynchester's fine sermons, which preach a message of uplifting yourself for God. This Minister dwelled on the evils to be found in man's soul.

But after, when we were walking back to our carriages, Mr Huntingdon casually mentioned, he would be taking his sister to Bath. They would be staying a couple nights with Mr Wynchester. In a few weeks I shall be seeing him again.

Later, we had a visit from my Uncle, Lord Wandesforde, and his wife. They came to say goodbye, and I was given the good news of a proposed visit from Maddy and Ned. With the season nearly over, Uncle wants them to have a chance to stay with people their own age (David and I). Cousin Julian will be escorting them and returning for them when it is time to deliver them home.

Can it be true? I will not be left to the sad plainness of existence, which I feared home would be after so much excitement here in the City.

We made an early night of it for we were leaving early in the day. I will have so much to tell David. How I long to see him.

26 June, 1820

Monday

We left in the morning. It was only listening to the Sammy and Delia chattering like magpies that I realised Mother had seen to their entertainment as well as Mine. Sammy and Delia went to the Royal Menagerie, a Museum and strolls in Green Park. They attended a circus. I almost envy them their pleasures, but mine were equally exciting if not so easily settled in my mind.

The journey home was better for Sammy being relieved of his pain, however Delia ate too large a breakfast and we had to make an unplanned stop to deal with her upset.

David met us in Newbury, and he had brought Nutmeg too. Papa agreed to my riding her home rather than spending another minute in the carriage. He even agreed to our going ahead, being accompanied by no other than a groom. It was heavenly, to race like the wind before bringing the horses to a walk. The groom kept far enough back to allow David and I private conversation.

I told him everything, though at first, I didn't mention my tangled emotions. Finally, he pressed me into confessing my feelings and after teasing me about it he did offer the information that my feelings were normal. He too has been taken by more than lady at a time. He refused to discuss who when I asked, but I saw the mischievous twinkle in his eye. I will learn more one day. He is pleased to hear of the abundance of company arriving soon, which will enliven his summer, for he finds the local village very flat for the most part. Though he has developed his friendship with the shy Mr Harry Hylton. He says Harry is quite fond of me. I blushed to hear this for I am sure I have done nothing to encourage him.

We arrived home, before the rest by some minutes and were settled inside by the time we were caught up with. Mother sent the children to bed, and she quizzed David most stringently on his activities in their absence. He gave her seemingly open answers, but I know his expression too well.

That night I found Misty in my room, she has grown so much in so little time. I swear she has grown quite three inches in height. She bounded happily around my room until Molly shut her out, fearing she'd make a mess in her excitement. I heard Mother yell at David for letting his puppy run wild but other than stuffing her in his room, he did nothing to attend to the problem. I think Papa will not let this situation go on much longer, he is a firm believer that dogs belong in the Kennel. Even to please mother, who wishes to please David, he will not let it continue.

The evening was quiet, and we ate plain food, or so it seemed after the exotic sauces and varied meats served in London homes. It looks like rain tonight and most likely tomorrow as well. I am glad I was able to ride even so little today for I fear riding will be out tomorrow.

27 June, 1820

Tuesday

It rained all day.

Mother set me back to the tasks which were interrupted by our London Idyll. I am for the next month completely in charge of the household. I will choose all menus. I will direct the Housekeeper and Cook. I will keep the accounts. I will also have to do all my normal tasks. Practising the piano, singing with Delia, Water-colours with David. Mending and finer stitchery. Reading to the family in the evenings. I do not know how I will do all this and not fall exhausted into my bed each day.

I chose the dinner menu. I am slowly learning, I think, which dishes go well together. Mama treated me to a smile after I presented the proposed menu to her. Papa sent his compliments to Cook, and I realised this was a one to me as well.

Already I have the menus planned for the rest of the week, but mother has warned me I have to be prepared to change them at the last minute if the Housekeeper cannot order the food I want. She has also told me it is important to take into account those foods which are in season. Those that are not, should be chosen for the menu sparingly and as a treat.

She explained: a wife's duty is to spend her husband's money responsibly. Every guinea spent needlessly is taken from your children's future. It is an odd thing to think of myself with children. But someday I think I would like to have several. Delia was an adorable baby, and I loved playing mother to her when Nurse would let me. Sammy was a little monkey but such a cheerful laughing baby. I hope my own children will have their good spirits and happy natures.

I think the rain has stopped. Perhaps if it is not too muddy, I will be able to ride Nutmeg in the morning.

28 June, 1820

Wednesday

It was cloudy in the morning, and David forecasted more rain. I could have done the same, but he likes to make his portentous prognostications.

I begged Mama to let us ride before the rain fell and I would attend to my practising later. With a deferential request on David's part, she submitted to our dearest wish, and we took out Nutmeg and Coriander.

We met with Harry who also was taking advantage of the break in the weather to gather sustaining fresh air. He was as delighted as Misty to see me. I could not stop blushing. He calmed by the time we parted and had our permission to visit upon the morrow.

The rest of the day was practice and accounts. Mother examined my stitchery and told me I needed smaller stitches. Bless me, but I do not see how I can make them smaller than they are.

Sammy fell from the lower branch of a tree, while out playing (having escaped Miss Horace's attentions) but fortunately the only damage was to his clothes. Very muddy he came back, grinning from ear to ear. Excited by the bird's nest he had found. It had one egg in it. I did not have the heart to tell him it would not crack without its mother to nurture it.

Lady Felicia sent me a letter, thanking me for coming to the Ball and for my congratulations on her new Marriage. She said she hopes I will correspond with her once she is settled in Australia, for it will be nice to have news of home and family. She embarks onto the Whistler's Fancy, at Portsmouth, on the 3rd. I wrote her back and said I would be delighted to avail myself of the opportunity to hear about all the exciting new places she would be seeing and felt my own humble tales of home would be small recompense. I sent it out with the other post, and she is certain to have it before she leaves. I may even hear back before she departs.

Life is very quiet, if busy now with all my responsibilities. I am getting a fuller portrait of Mother's life while attending to her duties. I never understood how much she does each day.

29 June, 1820

Thursday

I received a letter from Clementina Sherbourne today. She writes her brother still dances attendance upon Miss Sophia Warwicke. I find her words leave me with an impression she is not so enthused as she was previously with Miss Warwicke. Perhaps it is my own hopes which give me this impression.

Mother has informed me that my cousins will arrive in a week. I am to prepare the rooms for their stay. Maddy and Ned will be staying a month. Cousin Julian for a week to see them settled in and then to return for them at the end of their stay. During this time, I will be planning the entertainments. We will be offering a round of excitements for their amusement, and I will be inviting the neighbours to these pleasures. I am terribly excited with all this potential activity and frightened at the responsibility it will entail.

I spent the day discussing ideas for entertainments with any who would listen. Mrs Girling, Miss Horace, David, Mother, even Cordelia. I have designated the bedroom to my right to be Maddy's. I hope we will be like sisters. Much as love Delia, she is so much younger it is hard to share feelings and thoughts with her. And in our neighbourhood, there are few girls my own age. Often,

I have felt lonely, without a companion to visit. Ned will be set next to David, he has been more fortunate in finding friends both by being sent to school and being allowed to socialise with the lower classes in a way I am not. Still, he should enjoy Ned's presence in our house, someone in the evenings to play chess or piquet with. He plays them with me only reluctantly, saying I am sadly deficient in skill. But how can I when I have such infrequent practise?

So many plans whirl in my head, and many I know Mama will say are impractical. Tomorrow I must propose the entertainments I think she may agree to and then she will approve those she determines suitable.

Misty has been sent to the Kennels. Papa has decided the puppy is well enough grown she does not need especial attentions devoted to her. David was very unhappy at this decision but knew to expect it.

30 June, 1820

Friday

Mother has approved all my plans, with some small modifications but for the Masquerade ball I dreamt of holding.

She has explained the importance of pacing the events, leaving time open to rest and allow our neighbours to entertain us as well.

They will arrive on the fifth. We will dine *en famille*. The next day we will have a picnic. Already the Wynchesters have invited us and my cousins to dinner. On the 7th, we will attend the Dance in Newbury's Assembly Rooms. A dinner party on Saturday to properly introduce my cousins to the neighbourhood. Sunday will of course be a day of church and quiet activities.

The next week we will have a breakfast which will include the neighbours: Herrons, Buckminsters, Wynchesters, and some of the other families of the village (Mama has said I may invite Lady Peasedale and the D'Aubigny family, but she does not have expectations of their attendance). Later in the week, we will hold a musical evening for our friends and I to demonstrate our musical talents.

David proposed we perform a theatrical. He insists on choosing the piece. He intends to have Harry join as well and, if we need them, Mother has allowed that Delia and Sammy may join our efforts as well as the Buckminster children if their parents give permission. David will not tell me what he has chosen, but he assures me I will gain much enjoyment from performing it. Mother has asked for David's assurance it is a proper play. He affirms this but I see the mischievous twinkle in his eye.

Friday the 28th we will hold a grand formal ball. Mother is assisting me with the list of guests. We are inviting all the families of good standing within an evening's driving distance. A few will stay the night, but with our current guests, we will be limited in the number of bedrooms available for additional company. I will have the responsibility of hiring musicians. Oh, what if I choose badly? I have other plans, but Mama says nothing further need be written in stone.

Making plans, running the house, and practising my water-colours and piano filled my day quite handily. I had little time free for anything else.

1 July, 1820

Saturday

Delia and Sammy spent the day with Master and Miss Buckminster. I have set the servants to cleaning every inch of the house from attic to the men's servant quarters. Mrs Girling was horrified to find David's room infested with fleas and demanded to know every place Misty had been. She has torn everything out of his room and mine too (though there were not many to be found in mine - thank God!)

I was able to retrieve and hide this diary before she began dismantling my room.

Mother decided to hire help for the cleaning as we have so few days left. I spent the afternoon interviewing village women for the positions open. I chose the widow of one of our former tenant farmers and a cousin of Molly's. The cousin, Tabby, looks very like Molly. She is tall and thin, slightly taller than Molly. Mouse brown hair and pale blue eyes. Molly is the prettier I think, her features are more regular and her nose less snub.

Lately Sally has been sick frequently and others seem to spend inordinate amounts of time making up her work. I was going to speak to Mama, but David asked me to give her consideration, he says that I am being harsh on her because of what I saw, but I don't think it is true. The other maids do their work without all the fuss and complaints she makes. Her manner always has an insolent tone when she addresses me. Also, I know Molly does not like her. She mutters darkly when I mention Sally's name but will not speak openly to me. I am sleeping in the room which will be Maddy's while my room is scrubbed and rubbed to get rid of every one of those crawling pests. David has gone to spend the night at the Herrons, but I think this has more to do with the cockfight then his room. He cares less for such things than I do.

2 July, 1820

Sunday

Very quiet day. Church today. Mr Wynchester preached on the parable of the prodigal son. Perhaps fitting, Mother thought, as David neither returned home today nor attended church. She considers Mr Herron to be a vile influence upon David.

The restrictions on Sunday are often frustrating to my desire to finish projects, but one Mama feels it is important to keep the Sabbath day.

I wrote letters and, in the evening, we read from a book of improving essays. Mama feels it is important, especially in the face of our upcoming dissipation to remember what God wants from us. We had, Mama, Papa, Sammy, Delia and I, a discussion of the Ten Commandments and how they make our life better. I know I am sometimes guilty of a few (I am not always as pious as I should be on the Sabbath day, I do sometimes covet my neighbour's goods. David takes the lord's name in vain—I never have in anyone's hearing — Mother would simply expire) and regret my lapses.

An early night in keeping with the day. I am back in my own room tonight, blessedly. I missed my own bed.

3 July, 1820

Monday

We received a new device from London; a Patented Filtering Machine. It had been advertised in my Copies of La Belle Assemblée and Papa went to see it demonstrated, at the Western Exchange, during our excursion to the Metropolis. Papa is concerned about the purity of our water supply. He bought the largest machine, it filters 200 gallons a day.

After checking on the standing of various household tasks, Mama agreed I should take some fresh air. I went riding with Harry as David sent notice he was staying another night at the Herron's. Harry is a very sweet lad. He will speak on any topic I offer with alacrity and interest, yet I know fashions and poetry do not interest him. I have mentioned the play David will produce and asked if he would be willing to partake in it. He agreed with such enthusiasm; I cannot think his studies keep him fully occupied. He is very smart, so perhaps he doesn't feel the need to study excessively. He can speak and read both Latin and Greek fluently. He studies the sciences with a natural understanding. He tells me about his studies, I ask, and I learn much from him.

It is but a few days until the arrival of my Cousins. My excitement exceeds all my ability to support them calmly. Mother tells me to restrain myself and act my age. But I feel much as a five-year-old receiving [Christmas] gifts.

Dinner today, Chicken roasted, Leg of Mutton and Colliflower. I have asked the cook to vary the sauces, and she was extremely frightening when I did so. She held a large knife in her hand as she scowled at me until I nearly told her to not mind my request. But I do want to impress my Cousins, so I held my position and offered up several receipts which had been recommended to me (one from Mrs Wynchester - from the last dinner we attended. A very fine sauce.)

4 July, 1820

Tuesday

We have received notice. Maddy, Ned and Julian will be here tomorrow. My excitement is irrepressible. David has returned home. Mother lectured him severely on his delinquency from Church and has told him, if he cannot tend to his duties to the Lord, he shall not be spending the night from home again.

Papa tried to temper her words but did chastise David for forgetting his duties to his family and God. David appeared entirely repentant, but I am not one to believe that particular expression of innocent regret.

The cleaning of the house is nearly complete. Tomorrow will be Tabby and Mrs Cowen's last day. Mrs Cowen told me how much she appreciated the extra work and hoped we would keep her at mind if we needed additional staff in the future. She is in need of the additional income to help support her six children. Two are already working in other households but the youngest four are too young to be hired out yet. Her mother Mrs Ainsley tends to the children while she finds work. She takes in mending, does spinning and weaving and is praised by all who she has worked for. The only reason she has not found permanent employment is because she needs to be a day worker or abandon her family to her frail elderly mother's full-time care.

The rooms are all clean and aired. The wood glowing with beeswax polish. The chandeliers sparkling from the vinegar rinse. The silver is so shiny I can see myself, mirror sharp. The Washing has been done early, and all the linens are clean and the servants' uniforms extra tidy. All the servants have had a bath. Mother tells me I am going to an extreme, but I do so want our home to make a good impression.

Today I spent much of the day writing out the invitations for our ball. Mother has made me rewrite several of them because she felt they were not written finely enough.

Today, Cook made Mrs Wynchester's sauce. She did very well, and I am pleased with dinner. Papa praised it highly. David teased me but he ate much so I know he enjoyed it as well.

5 July, 1820

Wednesday

I woke early this morning. Lay listening to the hushed dawn. The light crept over the horizon and slowly the world came awake around me. The birds began to sing. I heard the servants moving around and Molly came to tend my room.

I was down to breakfast before anyone. I sat drinking my cocoa wondering if everything was done for my cousins' arrival. Papa joined me, placing a kiss on my head and telling me I looked very pretty. David showed himself next, he was in a foul humour. I told him to go back to his bed and come back when he had found a new face to show us. Papa laughingly agreed.

After breakfast, I went to talk to Mrs Girling. She guaranteed that everything was in order, took the menu changes I had made and assured me I was doing a fine job.

I was in fidgets the entire morning waiting for our guests. They arrived at two in an elegant equipage with outriders and fine liveried servants.

Mad Maddy nearly jumped out of the carriage before the steps were put down. She threw her arms around me with all the eagerness of a long-lost relative I had not seen for years rather than days.

Ned greeted me with nearly equal vociferousness but with slightly more decorum. Cousin Julian greeted me with all his fine manners. He kissed my fingers with practised elegance and declared me the prettiest thing he'd seen this month.

Laughter tickled my throat, but I held it back for his look contained all seriousness and it would be insufferable for me to laugh at his earnestness. We went inside and they greeted my parents before I showed them their rooms. David came out of his bedroom, showing a better humour than previously and dragged Ned off with him into the room next to his, set aside for my younger cousin. Next, I indicated Julian's room for his short stay and then took Maddy off to her room. Annie, her maid, was unpacking for her, Mrs Girling had been before me in showing the servants and my cousin's luggage to their respective rooms.

Dinner was a quiet affair, *en famille*. Julian was very complimentary of my *"well-chosen"* meal. Though he had no reason to know I was the one who had designed the menu.

Having Maddy here is so very exciting a prospect. To have someone to share my thoughts and feelings with!

After dinner, Papa read from Shakespeare and Cousin Julian read some of the sonnets to us. He has a lovely voice, very rich and smooth. He looked at me as he said the immortal bard's words. A frisson slid down my back as he gazed into my eyes.

Let me not to the marriage of true minds
Admit impediments. Love is not love
Which alters when it alteration finds,
Or bends with the remover to remove:
O no! it is an ever-fixed mark
That looks on tempests and is never shaken;
It is the star to every wandering bark,
Whose worth's unknown, although his height be taken.
Love's not Time's fool, though rosy lips and cheeks
Within his bending sickle's compass come:
Love alters not with his brief hours and weeks,

But bears it out even to the edge of doom.
If this be error and upon me proved,
I never writ, nor no man ever loved.

There is a knocking at my door, I think it is Maddy. Mother will so disapprove of us staying up to let our tongues have their full office as they could not before, but I have so much to tell her and so much to hear.

6 July, 1820

Thursday

I never would have guessed Maddy's secret heart ache. She is in love with a handsome young Lieutenant. One Denis Hammond of the 95th Foot, but her parents think she is too young, and he has not sufficient prospects to support a wife. She told me he has hair the shiny black of a raven's wing and eyes the colour of the sky at the heart of a storm. She is poetic in her description. She also assures me he does have prospects. His Uncle and God-father who bought him his colours is unmarried and has a fine little estate. His uncle has assured him, as soon as a suitable captaincy becomes available, he will be able to purchase up. But until her parents decide the son of a Viscount (who has been dangling after her) will not turn her thoughts to his direction, they will not accept Lieutenant Hammond's LOWER prospects as adequate and reasonable to maintain Maddy in her present lifestyle.

Maddy tells me she cares little about a society life. She would be quite content and happy to live the life of an Army wife. She has sworn me to secrecy and at the same time begged my assistance. She needs to be able to send Annie to the Village Inn regularly to pick up his letters and send hers. Oh, to have a man love me so passionately and faithfully.

Today was a whirlwind of activity. We all rose early though Maddy & I had not gone to sleep until past three.

We had a picnic by the Kennet, having invited the Wynchesters, the Buckminsters, and the Herrons, though mother frowned at Robert Herron, until he put himself out to charm her. She can resist him no more than the foolish young girls. Maddy flirted with him lightly, but I saw her send Annie off to the Inn and know she is having her check for the post.

Harry and Adam joined us as well.

Sammy and Gerry Buckminster found trouble for Adam to get into, but Mr Wynchester was very patient with him. Harry joined David, Ned, and Robert fishing. Robert Herron told us the news that his sister, Chloe was coming to stay in a sennight. She and her husband Mr Cavanaugh.

Delia and her friend Nichola Buckminster tagged after Maddy and I the entire afternoon until I begged Miss Horace to distract them.

That evening my cousins went to the theatre in Newbury with us. We saw a very amusing farce but what I remember most was Cousin Julian sitting beside me. His manner was most attentive and sincere in his admiration. It is most pleasant to have someone interested in my wellbeing and happiness at every turn.

I am most tired, and it does not appear that Maddy intends to come to my room to have a cosy night time chat. I must be glad for I am quite fatigued.

7 July, 1820

Friday

I slept late and did not wake until Maddy woke me with an urgent shake. She told me a ride was what we needed. I agreed and rang for Molly. Annie had David and Ned woken for us and we four took a turn into the village. Maddy conveniently needed to stop at the Inn and when she returned to our patient group, she had a cat in the cream expression on her face.

We returned to the house and she and I went to her room. She read the letter and then let me see it. She teased me for being so shocked to read the warm comments he directed to her. He tells her of his love in quite romantic terms, but I rather think Mother would consider him more shocking than Byron if she saw his words.

We dressed for our Dinner at the Wynchesters. It was a very pleasant meal and then it was off to the Assembly Rooms in Newbury. It was an excellent turn out —— quite 20 couples. I danced two waltzes and two country dances with Julian. I do like him very much. He is a gentle, kind, and considerate man. I danced twice with Ned, twice with Harry, once with Robert

Herron and one with his elder brother. We had a late supper which I went down to with Julian. Maddy and Robert joined us.

We did not get home until nearly four and I nearly fell into bed rather than write these words, but I feel to stop one night would lead to a ruinous laxity which would follow with many blank pages. I will not allow that to happen.

8 July 1820

Saturday

We were up so early. I feel like I barely had a moment's sleep. The house has been in such an uproar as the preparations take hold. Mrs Cowan and Tabby are back for today and all the male servants have been dressed in footman's livery and given basic lessons so they may help for the party. We have heard from all our neighbours, and they all are coming tonight.

My dress is laid out and I am writing this before I nap, as mother has insisted. I am too restless for sleep, but rest will be needed she says. Maddy is just as wild as I am for the evening to start.

Oh, it was such a delightful evening, and but for one mishap when the kitchen boy dropped the serving spoon in Mrs Buckminster's soup it went perfectly. Everyone admired the menu, and mother made it quite clear to our guests I was the planner and instrument of their pleasure.

After dinner the ladies had a lovely time exchanging gossip, and per mother's instructions father brought the men back to us soon.

We first had music. I played and Maddy sang. She has a very

nice soprano and knows all the latest airs. Living in London so much of the year, she knows all the current modalities. She had the loveliest lama silk which far outshone my simple white satin with tulle, elegantly ornamented with roses.

Julian assured me I was a diamond of the first water and more elegant by nature's handiwork than anyone else in the room. Miss Horace played for us and the footmen rolled up the carpet so we could dance. Julian immediately bespoke the first dance and the first waltz. I was in no position to refuse, even if I had so desired. As the daughter of the household, I danced with every man who wished it, and my feet show the wear from it. Harry stepped on my toes twice, but he was so eager for the dance and very much the fine gentleman tonight.

When the party broke up past two when the last guest left, Mama and Papa took me aside to tell me how proud they were of me. It will always be a treasured memory to know I could make them proud [of me].

9 July, 1820

Sunday

All I wanted was to sleep in after our busy and late night, but church could not be dismissed. Julian sat beside me and was most attentive to Vicar Wynchester. He complimented him afterwards for his thoughtful and admirable sermon. Mr Wynchester was nearly red with so much unexpected praise from such a fashionable London blade.

We returned home, and it was a quiet day. All in all.

We wrote letters and took turns reading *Persuasion* by Miss Austen. Such a sadness she died with so few books written, mother says they are excellent works and encourages us to read them when we will.

We had a pleasant dinner and played simple games in the evening. Julian leaves early in the morning. I will be sad to lose his fine companionship. He has added greatly to my enjoyment of my cousins' stay. He will be back in three weeks.

Maddy sent Annie off with a letter when we were at church, she did not show me this letter but of course I know it is for her Lieutenant.

Time for sleep, my eyes feel as if stones rest on them.

10 July, 1820

Monday

Julian set out the instant after breakfast. He told me only his attendance in town forced him from my side. He can be extravagant in his praise.

We had a quiet day, Maddy and I practised dancing with David and Ned. She sang while I played the Pianoforte. Delia is very jealous of our guests, she feels particularly out of sorts with everyone too busy for her. I'll have to make an effort to share more of my time with her. She is especially upset now that Sammy has received in invitation to stay with our Uncle Lord Welbourne.

We were invited to dinner at the Buckminsters for the evening. A pleasant evening and a fine dinner. Mother sent us to bed early with instructions [thinking we should] to catch up on our sleep while we might.

11 July, 1820

Tuesday

We have heard from the Countess of Peasedale, she and her married daughter will be attending tomorrow. Mama is simply in shock. She does not know what to make of this sudden familiarity. To think we will have a Princess in our home. The Countess' daughter married a Russian Prince. Nicholai Remiszovsky, such a romantic name! She met him when the Tsar visited in 1814. The Prince was in his retinue. This is the first time she has returned to England since their marriage. She has two children that have come with her. The elder is a boy and the babe, a girl.

Maddy and I went into Newbury to shop. She also stopped at the Inn in the village long enough for Annie to claim a letter. I believe she is trying to persuade him to elope with her. I do not know where her sense has gone. It simply is not the thing and even as the daughter of a Baron, she will find the consequences hard to bear. I am trying to work upon her reason to convince her it is not the done thing.

She helped me choose two new hats, gloves, and a parasol. With all the frolic planned, I will need the new items simply to keep my wardrobe from turning to rags.

Tomorrow is our Breakfast and again the house begins to resemble Bedlam as we attempt to order everything for the entertainment.

Maddy has sent off another letter to her Lieut. I believe I have convinced her to maintain discretion and decorum for now, but I do believe if she is too long thwarted, she will go the length of her tether and then break it.

I have so much to look forward to. I am fortunate indeed in my parents who have chosen to provide me with excellent society and a fine education to establish myself well. We read tonight. Maddy chose Miss Austen's *Northanger Abbey.* She has a fine cultivated reading voice.

12 July, 1820

Wednesday

My goodness, she is quite the finest and most elegant Lady I have ever seen. Princess Remiszovsky wore the most la mode attire. I am convinced it could only have come from Paris (I read my Fashion Magazines quite faithfully and can recognise the styles).

She was much sought after by our guests. Robert Herron was firmly put in his place when he tried to set up a flirtation with her. She had with her a Cossack as a servant. He was quite the cachet for our Breakfast. She also had a French woman to attend her two children. The two, both in leading strings, chattered in Russian and French with complete ease. Their Mama insisted they speak in English, but they continued to forget when not reminded. All the women were quite taken with the children and Delia ignored her friend, Miss Buckminister to play with them. She is very natural with small children and will, I do not doubt, make a superior mother.

Everyone agreed the Breakfast was a grand success. All were delighted with the privilege of meeting the little prince and princess and becoming acquainted/reacquainted with the ci-devant Lady Auriana D'Aubigny. The Countess was very gracious and assured us they would also attend our Musical on Friday and later our Ball. Mother is quite in a dither and has decided that she will have to take more of a hand in assisting me with the plans for the Ball.

After our guests left, we were still excitable for at least an hour, but then our evening was quite dull and stupid by comparison. It became an early night for us.

I found out David is sneaking Misty back into his room. She has grown to twice her previous size.

13 July, 1820

Thursday

David proposed our theatrical today. Harry could not join us as he had lessons but still is amenable to being in it. David insisted on Auditioning us! We still do not know what play he has chosen. He has had us act out various scenes from Shakespeare. Hamlet's Soliloquy, Beatrice, and Benedick's declaration of Love, Portia's defence of her beloved, Shylock's speech and Julius Caesar's death scene. Ned played that role with relish. Staggered about holding his stomach as if cruelly murdered as he gasped out *"Et tu, Brute?"*

Mother has become quite frenzied as she has spent her day rechecking all my plans to assure herself I did not overlook any detail for our Musical Evening.

Maddy and I spent most of the day practising our performances for the morrow. We have several performers who will be playing. Maddy and I will play separately and in duet. Also, we will have Mrs Buckminster who plays very well. Miss Horace will play while Mrs Winchester sings. She has the finest voice in our neighbourhood. David, and Harry have agreed to sing. Ned refused with the claim he has no voice. David assured me it was the full and complete truth. Mrs Chloe Cavanaugh nee Herron will play and sing. The Princess has agreed to sing, and her Cossack will also perform a small demonstration of his native dancing and singing.

It is quite the coup. We do not know how we came to receive such an honour but will gladly make free to enjoy it.

After dinner, David and I played Chess against Ned and Maddy. This was an odd way to play for the team who had finished their move must leave the game table and allow the two whose turn it was to plan strategy. Ned and Maddy were very argumentative over their moves and David and I could hear their strategy, unsurprisingly we won.

It rained much of the day, but lightly enough the roads are not all mud. It is hoped it will dry by tomorrow evening.

14 July 1820

Friday

The evening was an unparalleled success or so everyone told me. Maddy and I started the evening's performances and from there we heard such lovely songs and voices. But the finest moment in our evening must be the Princess singing a Russian Love song. It was beautiful and haunting. That and her Cossack who was frighteningly fierce and aggressive in his dancing. I felt positively vulnerable under his menacing gaze as he scowled from under thick eyebrows while dancing. Maddy was only amused by him and tried to speak to him. He speaks no English, but a little French and therefore she had to have the Princess translate for them both during their conversation.

We partook of a midnight supper and Miss Horace played for us. We made up ten couples for dancing. I am quite tired and long for sleep and yet the evening spins through my head quite active and will not allow for rest. I must try, for tomorrow we ride out, early, with several gentlemen of the neighbourhood and Mrs Cavanaugh too. We will visit Newbury for there are to be some informal races to attend. Mama was reluctant to allow it until Mrs

Cavanaugh agreed to be our Chaperone. Is it not funny that she is a little older than I, but marriage makes it all acceptable.

To sleep. Or as Shakespeare would have us say it "*sleep, perchance to dream.*"

15 July, 1820

Saturday

Oh my, what a very fine day we had. We rode out the Newbury and who should we meet up with? Mr Cole Huntingdon and his sister, Mrs Sheffield. He is taking her to Bath for her health. She is not a very good traveller, and they will rest in Newbury a couple days while she recovers. She was lying down in the care of her maid therefore we had the pleasure of Mr Huntingdon joining us. I won my wager having picked the right horse for the first race. Mr Huntingdon had me choose his horses for the remaining races and all but one of them won. I do not know if I do have a talent for picking *"the horses"* as he claims or if I was exceptionally fortunate in my choices.

Mr Huntingdon could not come back with us, but he did promise to call upon Eldridge House at the first opportunity to give his regards to my parents.

Maddy sees with clear eyes for she noticed my interest within but a moment. She rallied me quite fiercely about it and yet I could tell her little for my feelings are much confused. Her brother Julian enchants me with his elegance and wit and obvious interest, but Mr Huntingdon touches something within me. When I am with him, the world seems to fall away, and I wish for nothing but his presence. And finally, there is Mr Sherbourne who makes my heart beat so fast I feel as if I will faint. I look at him and feel completely under his spell. And yet he shows equal or more interest in Clementina's friend, Miss Warwicke. It is very pleasant to be admired and most painful to know someone you esteem admires someone else more.

Maddy received another letter from her Lieut. She has not persuaded him from his honourable course yet and I do hope he will stand firm.

16 July, 1820

Sunday

Mr Huntingdon and Mrs Sheffield were in church today. Mama showed them every courtesy and invited them back to the Eldridge House rather than to immediately partake of a journey back to Newbury. I am sure they could have attended a church there, but Mr Wynchester would have undoubtedly taken it ill if they had not attended his service. It was an excellent sermon based on the Sermon on the Mount. I do think Mr Wynchester quite the finest Minister I have had the pleasure of hearing speak. His curate is not nearly so well spoken or comprehensive in his understanding of the bible. Mr Wynchester is a man who wishes to uplift his fellow man to heaven. The curate appears to be willing to cast the majority of the congregation down to the burning pits.

Mr Huntingdon and I took a turn in the park and talked so long, Maddy was finally sent out to find us. Mrs Sheffield seemed unperturbed by our absence but equally desirous of leaving when given the opportunity. It would seem she was not feeling well. This is a symptom of her delicate condition.

The day was quite stupid after that. We began practising the play. Harry was able to join us for the day, so we had the full complement to begin practice of the play. I do not know how Mother will feel about David's choice of play, but he is doing his best to keep his selection quiet until the last moment.

We read after dinner. The weather was chilly for summer.

17 July 1820

Monday

Maddy received another letter from her officer. She did not let me read this letter, so I fear the worst. I am attempting every remonstrance I can to keep her from foolhardy actions. We practised the play for much of the afternoon. Molly, whose reading has improved immensely with my weekly lessons, read Harry's part for he was not able to join us today. After practice I spent some time tending to the house's concerns. Maddy answered her letter and sent Annie off to the village. I worry I should tell Mama, so she may keep Maddy from consequences which will haunt her til her days' end but do not feel capable of betraying her at this time.

Mr Huntingdon and his sister joined us for dinner. Ned and David dragged Mr H. off to play billiards while the ladies stayed in the Parlour to talk. Mrs Sheffield was most kind to me and spoke to me of many subjects but most often of her brother. She believes him to have a great future in front of him. He has been prepared for a career in the Diplomatic corps by the wish and will of his parents.

I can see this career would suit him for he has the finest

manners and most honest face I have seen. Mr H. joined us while I was playing the piano. He chose to sit beside me and turn pages while I played. I did not need them turned, but prized his presence beside me.

18 July, 1820

Tuesday

Mr H. and his sister, Mrs S. took their leave of us, but Mr H. promised he would return for the Ball. My happiness must be complete for I have promised him my hand for a waltz and the supper dance.

We practised the play quite half the afternoon, after a ride out in the late morning. Ned has become decidedly flirtatious with Mrs Cavanaugh who we met with on our outing. She is quite five years older than him and it appears most ridiculous to my eyes. Maddy is in full agreement with me and harassed him fiercely.

We have received an invitation to a Masquerade Ball at Bellewicke, to be held by Lady Peasedale in honour of her daughter's visit. Lord and Lady Bellewicke will be there as well. Many of the Ton will be coming from all counties to attend. I am so very excited by the prospect. After seeing the Invitation, Maddy immediately wrote a letter to her parents to beg their stay be extended. She is certain of her Mother's consent, who would refuse the opportunity for their daughter to attend a Ball at the Countess's fine home. Bellewicke Manor is considered one of the Premier homes in England. Tomorrow Maddy and I will be going to Newbury with Mama to choose costumes.

Maddy just left my chamber, she was so excited to discuss who we should be. I wish to be Empress Josephine at her Coronation. I have always loved that delightful costume from the many prints which have been published and of the painting done by David. So grand and beautiful! Maddy wants to be Cleopatra. I do not think it the most original choice, but she is quite determined upon it.

19 July 1820

Wednesday

Mother reminded me to attend to household concerns before we left for Newbury. Mother had chosen a dress in the style of the wife of a Roman Senator. She took a sketch to the Modiste to show her exactly what she wanted. What design and trim. I took with me all the drawings and details I could find for Josephine. Maddy had David sketch her idea of Cleopatra and though the Dressmaker now has the commission, it must wait upon permission from her mother to commence.

We did not arrive back until far into the afternoon. We found David and Ned fencing in the Hall. Papa was watching them, calling out suggestions. They were quite clumsy and Maddy insisted we be allowed to try. Papa coached us as well. I beat Maddy most handily but lost to David. He had the advantage of arm length on me and the lack of skirts encumbering him.

Dinner was a quiet affair. Maddy helped me sort through the acceptances for our Ball. While in Newbury I bought new trim for my gown from London. I am determined to make it over so it will look different than it was before. I began planning where my trim would go to best effect.

20 July, 1820

Thursday

Maddy is on pins to hear from her Mother.

We practised the play today, Papa came and watched for a short while. I think he was amused by David's choice. Therefore, it is hoped if mother wishes to banish it, he will overrule her. It is rare he interferes with domestic concerns but sometimes he will suggest to mother our behaviour is harmless.

Papa is truly the best of fathers. He went riding with us today. David and Ned hung on his every word as he spoke of current world concerns. Maddy showed less interest, but I tried to listen to him through Maddy's chatter.

We practised the play without Harry again, Molly does his role quite fine.

Papa read to us after dinner. He reads with distinction, each character living in that moment he spoke their words.

21 July, 1820

Friday

David and Ned went to stay for a couple days with Robert Herron at some hunting lodge of a friend of his. Mama was (quite) unwillingly to agree but Papa overrode her. The house seems quite quiet without them.

Sally was sick again today. I do believe if she does not improve her health (as if I believe her tales of fever and weakness—though Mrs Girling says her wash basin showed signs of illness and her forehead very clammy this morning) I will discuss with Mama her departure for Michaelmas. It is insupportable how little work she does, malingering in bed.

Tomorrow we are to go to Newbury to hire the musicians for the Ball.

We have been invited to the Buckminsters for dinner Monday.

Maddy and I drove into the village with Annie to attend us. I bought a Castilian blue bonnet of the Village shape. Maddy purchased a turban which took her deepest fancy, nothing I could say gave her discouragement. And though they are quite the mode, unfortunately this style does nothing for her appearance. We each bought a new parasol of the current style, wide fringe with balls hanging from them, as reported in La Belle Assemblée. I purchased one in lilac which will complement many of the shades in my present wardrobe. Maddy a Canary yellow. She has a fondness for bright colours that would become me ill, but look delightful on her stronger colouring. Hair of ebony brown and slate grey eyes. We both purchased plain silk handkerchiefs to embroider. What with David's birthday in August and Ned and Maddy's in September we both have presents to prepare. I purchased fabric and plan to make a ridicule for Maddy. I will stitch it with her Monogram and her Lieutenant's. She will love it even if she cannot show it to anyone for some time longer.

22 July, 1820

Saturday

It was a long day in Newbury. We saw several groups of musicians and finally chose one with a very handsome violinist. Maddy was quite flirtatious with him when Mama was not near us. I do think Maddy would flirt at a 60-year-old matron, it is simply her nature.

We have also ordered many specialty dishes to be delivered for the Ball. Ices, slivered ham, Champagne ordered. I do believe our ball must be a success. Few have turned down our invitations, mostly those who are sick or have gone to Scotland early for the Grouse shooting so popular there.

We have heard from Maddy's Mama who said they wished to come as well, but they are held in London on the King's business. She has said Maddy will be able to return for the Peasedale Masquerade (with Julian as escort), but she and Ned must still return to London on the scheduled date. I am quite disappointed to not have her longer with us.

Maddy and I spent much of the day sewing initials on the handkerchiefs. We had Molly read to us. She is learning to put feeling into her voice as she reads. At first, she sounded quite dead when she read out loud.

Maddy and I went down to the kitchen. She helped me brave the Cook and explain about the dishes we have ordered. She was very offended but with Maddy's talent for persuasion we ended with her convinced we were doing this for her, and it was merely because we do not wish to work her to death.

This is something for me to learn from Maddy, she has a natural ability to connect with people of all ages and position in life. She has agreed to go with me tomorrow after church to take baskets to the farmers who are experiencing hardships. We spent much of the evening after dinner preparing them.

23 July, 1820

Sunday

The sermon today was very well done. Mr Wynchester outshone himself. Harry came with us to help deliver our baskets. He was very sweet in helping us distribute them. Maddy was very good to our failing tenants. I think she would make a very good Viscountess someday, but I know she is determined to marry her Lieutenant.

As we were nearly finished delivering our charitable endeavours, it began to rain very hard. We returned to Eldridge House with Harry where he had to borrow clothes from David while his dried. He looked quite comical in David's much longer clothes, but he joined us in the Parlour while we worked on our stitchery. He was very complimentary and assured us of his discretion in the matter of our relatives' birthday gifts. We sent a groom to inform Mr Wynchester that Harry would be spending the night, as the weather continued to worsen as the evening progressed. He was quite embarrassed to be invited/required to stay and was most willing to return home in the deluge of rain falling down upon Berkshire. He was very shy at dinner and for the remaining portion of the evening before mother sent us all to bed early. In this case, Maddy was less than helpful as her flirtatious manner left Harry blushing and speechless every time she addressed him.

24 July, 1820

Monday

Maddy and I finished our handkerchiefs. We went riding to *"escort"* Harry home. He was quite delighted to be the sole company of two *"pretty"* ladies.

David and Ned are to return tomorrow. Mother has been muttering about the evils of the house party they are attending, without knowing anything about it. She appears to be assuming the worst is happening which will corrupt her son's moral and mental centres. I would never undeceive her about the state of her son's innocence.

We had a very fine dinner at the Buckministers. They have a Fancy French Chef, not plain English cook for them. The desserts were quite amazing. Maddy and I had too many of these treats but could not resist them. We played cards after dinner. The Buckministers and my parents played Whist, while Maddy and I played Piquet. We played for love, as neither of us wished to waste our substance on the other.

Four more days to our Ball. Oh, I cannot wait! Maddy is equally excited, and we both look forward to dancing with the many young men who have been invited. The local boys have all put in their bids for dances and Maddy despite her secret betrothal has every intention of enjoying their attentions.

25 July, 1820

Tuesday

David and Ned are home. They are quite worn from their dissipation and after greeting us slept the day away. Quite useless the two of them. Everything is madness as we prepare for the ball. We have in extra servants again. The gardeners are getting quick lessons in being footman and having outfits fitted to them. Tabby and Mrs Cowan are back to help Mrs Girling. Sally was sick again this morning. I sincerely believe she is Malingering. I believe Mrs Girling feels as I do, but she will not discuss it with me. I will have to go to mother but after the Ball, I want nothing to disturb the ball.

David and Ned were up for dinner. Mother questioned David closely after dinner about his time with Robert Herron. He refused to answer anything past enjoyment of dinners and steeple chasing across the countryside.

After dinner Mother and I went over the tasks which still needed to be overseen. She again checked over the menu for those foods Cook will be preparing. She too will have extra help for the next few days.

Tomorrow Maddy and I need to go to Newbury for a fitting on our costumes. Maddy received another letter which she again would not show me. I am worried.

26 July 1820

Wednesday

Too tired to write much.

Harry came over briefly to ride. I could not ride long, so Maddy and I returned while the boys continued without us.

Plans are nearly complete, invitations continue to arrive. Uncle Hugh, Lady Welbourne, Cousins Spencer, and Edmund arrive tomorrow as well as Uncle Lewis and Aunt Clytie. I have confirmed their rooms to be fully aired and prepared for them. Mama's godson Philip Royce-Collier will arrive the morning of the ball. I have not seen him for many years. He had bright red hair, but that is all I remember.

Rained in the afternoon. Dinner was a little overcooked, I think Cook is nervous.

27 July, 1820

Thursday

Philip arrived early, and yet late. He arrived a day early, but not until after dinner was on the table. He is a year older than David. But looks older. He is very distinguished despite his vibrant auburn hair. I swear it has fire within it, yes, I am being fanciful, but it is quite compelling to watch the firelight reflect upon it.

We had a very quiet day in social activities but very busy for plans. All the last minute arrangements came crashing down on us. Mama had Maddy and I check each bedroom for its readiness for guests. Maddy will be staying in my room for the night and so will Ned in David's as we will need the bedrooms for our overnight guests.

We practised our dancing in the Evening. Philip was very pleased to get some practice in as he said he was rusty. I saw no evidence of this as he was pronounced by both Maddy and I that his steps were quite competent and we looked forward to seeing him at the ball.

It is early, for mother has insisted we will need our sleep, but it is so very hard to rest knowing what tomorrow will bring.

Oh, how I look forward to tomorrow.

28 July, 1820

Friday

I know my Midsummer's dream. It all came to me the moment I saw him. The man I love. I wanted to tell him, but could not be so forward.

It seems a dream, the ball. Everything was so perfect and unencumbered with problems I do not believe I can ever have a more perfect occasion.

I must tell it in order, or my words will make no sense, my head spins, and whirls much as I did the whole of the night. Dawn has long gone, but these words must be writ, or I will lose the essence of my feelings.

We had dinner first with those spending the night. Uncle Lewis was dashing in his regimentals. It gleams and glitters with all his decorations. Aunt Clytie, of the Cambridge Malvernes, is a most elegant creature and yet the friendliest soul I know. She never speaks to a person without bringing a smile to his face. She is not beautiful so much as handsome and is a tall willowy creature who stands above the usual crowd.

I sat next to Philip at dinner, he kept me entirely amused with his banter and recounting of his adventures. Many of which I am sure are highly expurgated, as some hint at things I am not allowed to know.

Soon the ball began, I do admit my eyes kept straying to the end of the line, looking for one particular person. I greeted person after person until my knees were ready to creak and my hand felt useless to the task of greeting another person. And then it was him.

He looked so very handsome. His eyes more blue than I remembered. The deep rich azure of heaven's gate. His honey brown hair looked soft and touchable. I wanted to feel it. The look in his eyes told me, before his warm voice could, how lovely he thought I looked.

I felt faint with the sudden heat of the room, I nearly put a hand out to him to walk away with him then, but I was recalled to the remnants of the line and after agreeing to dance with him, allowed him to pass into the ballroom.

I danced the first dance with Lord Bellewicke who complimented me on my fine appearance. Papa danced with the Countess. She was delighted with his presence. Her husband, Sir Gabriel Ravenspur, danced with Mama, perhaps an improper choice of partner as he does not share his wife's status, but Mama said she would rather open with him than her brother. In the country, it is easier to bend the rules of protocol, but she told me it is essential to always know them, or you may break them when you should not.

Lady Bellewicke was returned to her husband, and she smiled at me and spoke kindly then the world disappeared. All I could see was him, coming to claim his dance. And my dream, fell into place. It was here. This moment in time. I do not know what I may have said if anything to the couple at my side. I only remember following him onto the dance floor and swirling to the music. I blush to remember it now, but then I cared only for his arms holding me with gentle firmness. I felt such belonging in his embrace. I know not if I spoke a single word, nor him. I only remember what his eyes said to me, and what mine must equally have said to him.

Our idyll ended too soon and again I had to attend to the guests. I danced every dance, my eyes straying to him every moment they could. Finally, he arrived to escort me to supper. I ate something. It was ambrosia as he put it on a plate for me. We talked. He told me about his plans. He is being considered for a new post in the government. I cannot be but proud for him. Someone so young, advancing so fast on talent rather than his connections. He is fortunate to have both, but it is clear he advances on abilities.

Maddy found time to tease me for my interest. But she assured me it would only be obvious to those who know me well.

I danced with many other gentlemen, of varying skill. My slippers are quite ruined. Harry stepped on my toes twice.

Eventually, the dawning sun was streaming though the paned windows, the candles down to the stubs, and it was time for the last dance. He was there at my side, and took my hand, placing it on the smooth superfine of his jacket. I could feel the living warmth of him.

I cannot sleep for thought of him. He is the one I was meant for. No other could make me happy as he would. I think he feels the same. He is a fine man who would never speak improperly, but surely eyes cannot lie.

29 July, 1820

Saturday

I was very tired when I woke. Only four hours of sleep. So much work to be done, making sure the mess from the ball was cleaned. Maddy was sweet and helpful. We had guests to entertain in the home, which fortunately meant they too were tired and slept late. Sally looked very ill, but she did work. Very little work, but she did work.

Callers began to arrive. Mr Huntingdon was one of the first among them. He asked me for me to accompany him for a drive, which I sadly had to refuse. But Mother did invite him to join us for dinner. I was so entirely relieved I knew he must see it.

The middle part of the day fell into an abyss in my memory, it was not until dinner that I again came to life. I wore my pretty blue gown, and Mr Huntingdon complimented me on my fine appearance. I was seated between Philip Royce-Collier and my Uncle Lewis. Maddy opposite me, was seated next to Mr Huntingdon. I did not know I could feel such a bundle of jealousy as she flirted with him, as she does with every man. I wanted him to myself.

After dinner, I was asked to play the piano, and I got my wish, he insisted on turning the pages for me. Which perhaps I needed as

I stumbled several times, unable to concentrate on anything but him. Finally, Maddy took a turn and he and I sat by the empty fireplace talking.

He asked me so many questions about my life, he shows a determined interest in me that warms my heart. He will be at church tomorrow, but Mama would not approve of my driving out with him tomorrow. Instead, we are going riding on Monday. He has promised to stay through the week. Fortunately, Mr Wynchester regards his godson highly, or I would be deprived of his presence.

30 July, 1820

Sunday

Mr Wynchester preached on the Glory of Heaven and why we want to be deserving of God's love. Unfortunately, in that moment, I was most sacrilegious for the only Glory I seek is to be in Mr Huntingdon's arms. The only love I seek, his.

The sermon was too long and too short. Too long for I had no ears for it, too short in that I never wanted to leave Mr Huntingdon's presence. I yearn to have him look at me as he did last night. I yearn to dance once more with him.

I now understand Maddy more fully. I cannot but want to be with him, as she wants to be with her Lieutenant. I fully understand the suffering she labours under with her cheerful smile and casual flirtation. I yearn to be in his presence, to bask in his smile, to hear his voice, saying Anything so long as he is speaking to me.

Most of our guests left for their homes after church, but Philip is still with us. He, David and Ned are going off with Robert Herron tomorrow. Mother was only persuaded by the most determined pleas on their part. I do not believe mother will ever approve of Mr Herron.

Maddy was feeling unwell this evening, and she is back in her own room being attended by her maid. Mama said I could still go on my ride with Mr Huntingdon, as long as I took a groom. I could barely restrain my gratitude to her, for losing my chance to be with him, would surely have broken my heart.

31 July, 1820

Monday

I sit here with only one thought in my mind. Mama noted my distraction at dinner, but I could not tell her. I did not dare even tell Maddy. Maybe I would share David if he was here, but he sent note they were staying in Newbury for the night.

Cole arrived, and we went to the stables. Jemmy saddled Nutmeg for me and Coriander for himself. Cole rode a handsome black gelding with a white blaze and three white socks. We rode up towards the fields past tall grain and reached open pasture. Without another word we knew an all-out gallop was what we needed. We raced along the edges of the trees forgetting to note if Jemmy kept up. We rode and rode only slowing down when we reached the woods. I gave him a challenging look, and he followed me down the path cut through the trees to a favourite spot for Delia and me to pick berries and flowers.

I don't know what happened, it must have been a hole dug by some animal. And I must be glad we were not moving fast, for Nutmeg stumbled and threw me. I was stunned. I could not breathe for several long painful moments. When I opened my eyes,

I had proof of his affections. It was a moment that will live enshrined forever in my heart.

We reached the edge of the woods, and Jemmy found us. Fortunately, I was able to brush off the ground's ill effects from my habit for I did not want Mama or Papa to know of my accident.

I wanted Cole to be able to join us for dinner, but Mama would have been horrified if I invited him. I know he must have seen the wish in my eyes. He is to take me for a drive tomorrow. The morning cannot come soon enough.

My heart sings his name. There truly can nothing so wonderful in this world and beyond as this feeling.

Addendum

(WHAT HAPPENED WHEN I FELL OFF NUTMEG...)

I must write it here on a separate sheet of paper - I do not dare to put it in my diary.

When I opened my eyes, Cole was holding me in his arms. His face was a mix of panic and love. He loves me! Before I could speak, after regaining breath, I was pressed close to his heart, murmurs of *'My dearest, my beloved,'* escaped him, then he was kissing me. It was terrifying at first, his lips pressed so desperately against mine, but he pulled away and I cried out against it, for I didn't want him to abandon me.

He touched my face as if I were the most precious thing he had ever beheld. *"Oh, my love, are you all right?"*

I could not speak but nodded. He caressed my cheek and gazed at me with his beautiful eyes. He brought his mouth back to mine, and I know nothing will compare to the feelings which filled me in that moment. His lips were tender as he held me close to him, they moved against mine filling me with this restlessness. I was as wanton as a dairy maid holding him to me, never wanting him to let me go. I do not know how long we stayed like this, me in his arms, him pouring his love over me, like Gilead's balm.

Reassured I was well, he lifted to me to my feet and stepped away. His face was quite flushed. He apologised and begged my forgiveness. I began to cry, I couldn't help it; how could he apologise for loving me? I found myself back in his arms. He patted my back as awkwardly as David used to when we were children out playing and I would get hurt and cry.

But I didn't want to be treated like a child. I do not believe I did what I did next, not that I regret it. I put my arms around his neck and pulled his head to mine and KISSED him. At first, he seemed to resist my touch, but when I pressed myself closer, he lost his restraint and our third kiss was so magical so wondrous, I never wanted it to end. It did, but this time he made no apologies.

He was quiet on our return to Eldridge, but his eyes spoke most eloquently for him.

He has promised to take me for a drive; I want so to be with him always. There is nothing else I want anymore. Not balls, not parties, not the world. I want to share his life, his thoughts, his joys, his dreams; I want to be the woman with whom he can share his sorrows and his pains. There is nothing more I can ask for.

1 August, 1820

Tuesday

My heart is desolate. I fear mother may suspect something. Cousin Julian returned today and somehow my drive out with Cole was changed to a party of four. Maddy and Julian accompanied us. We had not a moment to speak our hearts to each other. Cousin Julian is one of the sweetest men I know, but I wanted none of his company if it deprived me of Cole's. Maddy insisted we drive into the village, and we made a stop at the inn. I saw the letter she tucked into her reticule. If I told her, would she help me?

I must talk to him, hear him speak for me alone, and not with words meant for all.

It is fortunate we had not yet invited people to see our play, mother took one look at our practice and banned our continuance. No words from Papa could move her. She and David fought quite fiercely until Papa had no choice to send David to his room.

Dinner was long, dinner was lonely, dinner was nothing without Cole. I could barely eat for my desire to be with Cole. I cannot bear to be without him. I need to hear him say he loves me, once again. It has been too long.

2 August, 1820

Wednesday

All us young people went to the Abbey to explore the ruins. Ned and David, Cousin Julian, and Maddy and Harry and Cole.

We explored and walked around and had a picnic. I was desperate for a moment alone with Cole and begged Maddy to help me, though I did not explain all the circumstances. There was a sheltered spot in the Abbey and as we all played a game of sorts to see who could find the most interesting item, we departed in pairs.

When we were alone, Cole touched my face as if I was the most fragile china, stroking along my cheekbone as if I were a mirage. "*You are so beautiful,*" he told me. I smiled my joy but was speechless in the face of his adoration. I put a hand to his heartbeat, and it was as fast as mine was.

"*You are so lovely, so young... I can't... Beatrice, it's too...*" He seemed incapable of finishing any of his thoughts. "*I want you to ...*" I thought I was to hear the words I wanted most to hear, and instead we were interrupted. I did not have another moment alone with him.

Why, oh why, did Ned and Harry have to come upon us at that moment?

When we parted ways at the Vicarage, Cole gave me such a look of longing that I was sure I would expire with happiness.

The Wynchesters were invited to dinner, so I had the happiness of Cole's company for dinner. Sadly, I had Cousin Julian on one side and Ned on the other, but at least I was able to gaze upon him as he watched me through dinner. Every minute with him is a joy. Sometimes a painful joy because I know it must end, but I will not give up one moment of my time with him.

I played the pianoforte after dinner and had two men to help me turn the pages, two too many for my actual need. One too many for my want.

3 August, 1820

Thursday

My unhappiness knows no bounds. Cole left this morning. The pain of being apart from him is unbearable. My heart feels as if it has been torn asunder, for it has gone with him and left me empty. I was rude indeed, but I told Mother I had a headache and retired early. I cannot bear to pretend to be happy when I have no smiles left.

Molly has just handed me a missive. It is from my own dear Cole. My darling man found a way to bribe this message to be delivered to Molly. A risky venture, but I am so glad he did. To hold this letter close to my heart, almost makes his absence bearable. I have read it a dozen times and each time makes my feelings grow stronger for him.

Addendum

Cole's Letter

Dearest, I cannot regret more that I must leave. There is so much I did not say. So much I should have said. I carry you in my heart. I will return as soon as I may, but I have affairs I must attend to in London.

Every moment away from you will be as a thousand years. My world is a wasteland without you here with me. I know I say too much in this letter, and I apologise for my forwardness, but I cannot leave you without expressing some small part of what I feel.

It will be some time before I can return.

Please keep yourself well and happy in my absence. I wish more than anything to know you are filling your days with delight and joy until my return.

I will hear of you, I am sure, from my God-father's letters and will write him faithfully in the hopes you will hear of me.

Yours respectively and sincerely,

Cole

4 August, 1820

Friday

I am sad the Achertons Cousins have left but mother has a surprise indeed for me. Mama received a letter from Lady Sherbourne yesterday and has sent a response today. Clementina has been in Scotland, and she was to return to her family this week, however Freddy has the measles, and Lady Sherbourne does not want her to return home. Mama thought there would be nothing better to soothe my loss of the Achertons Cousins as to have Clementina visit.

I am trying to be mindful of my Cole's words and look forward to the coming days instead of regretting his absence. It is hard, but for him I will be happy.

Cousin Julian made it very clear that he had no wish to depart. Maddy hugged me fiercely and promised me she'd write. There is something in the way she said this that concerns me deeply. I fear what she and her Lieutenant will do, even if I now understand her feelings of desperation. Ned was happy to leave for he has said many times to David London has many more exciting places to keep him entertained.

Mama has set me back to my practising while our company is

gone. She has also said my household duties have suffered and I must pay more attention to them. I know she speaks the truth and can only make myself do them with the reminder that Cole will want a wife who can manage a proper house. Everything I do is for Cole. To be what he wants and needs.

5 August, 1820

Saturday

Cordelia fell from her horse. She is concussed, the doctor says and has a broken leg. She is in a great deal of pain. The household is topsy-turvy as a result. I do not know why her illness seems to have such an effect. David did not rouse such concern, nor do I. But the servants seem to try to find a way to ask after her or to be near her room. I have neglected her terribly of late, engrossed in my own concerns. I have dedicated myself to her. I will tend to her needs for as long as she requires me.

I have been a bad sister and have much to make up to her. I am here in my bedroom now only because mother insisted I return to bed and so I write this note.

Poor Delia. I have sent for books from the circulating library which I hope will please her most. Mama is teaching me how to tend to her. She has shown me how to prepare lavender water to soothe her brow, barley water to wet her dry throat. What to say to soothe her when the doctor wishes to leech her. Delia so dislikes this she became nearly hysterical. Poor dearest Delia. She looks so small and fragile in the bed, her leg braced against movement.

Tomorrow, I hope to convince mother to let me bring one of the kittens in to keep her company. She so loves animals. Maybe even Misty, except Misty is still boisterous and infinitely larger and might hurt Delia in her enthusiasm.

6 August, 1820

Sunday

I am terribly tired, poor Delia was quite fretful. Nothing eased her pain, except large doses of Laudanum. Still, she was restless, and I needed to keep her from doing further damage to her injured limb.

I read to her, I wiped her brow, I told her funny stories. Everything irritated her nerves rather than soothing them.

We went to church, while Mama stayed with Cordelia. I found no peace in church my thoughts torn between my memories of Cole so closely tied to Mr Wynchester and Delia's unhappy situation.

The day was rainy, and a Lightning storm woke her from her Uneasy slumber. Delia is terribly frightened by thunder and cried most pitifully. I won from mother the Concession of a kitten to pacify her fretfulness. I had every intention of going to choose one for her, but Molly insisted on doing the task for me. She picked a tiny little ball of tortoiseshell fluff. So sweet. It purred and licked my hand as I took it to Delia. She was so delighted she quite forgot to cry as the storm continued as loudly as a battle.

The rain continues, but the cacophony has passed. Delia fell into a deep sleep, not a half hour past and finally I may rest as well.

7 August, 1820

Monday

The doctor bled Cordelia again today. She was so very unhappy, but bravely she cried not at all. She slept nearly the entire day after this. I read to her and tended to her. I sang her songs. I held the kitten so she could pet it.

She is a dear little sister and deserves better from me. I am determined to be less selfish in the future.

Mrs Wynchester came to visit and had news from Cole. He has written twice since he left, she was surprised by the frequency of his correspondence. She has no idea how desperately I was waiting for even this small drop of news. It seems he will soon receive his promotion. The work he is involved in is clearing up those tasks of his old position before he leaves it for the new. He is an honourable man to work so hard to leave the post free of old tasks. He is a man I may be proud of.

How I miss him. I read his note every morning, every night. I carry it next to my heart wrapped in a piece of silk. I wish him here.

I nearly forgot to tend to the airing of the rooms for our guest's arrival. Clementina is to be escorted by Mr Sherbourne, and he will stay for the Peasedale Masquerade. I am torn between my wicked desire to attend the masquerade and my duty to Delia. I also will be able to see Maddy again and perhaps I can determine what actions she is contemplating. I am very concerned by her letter which I received today, which was vague regarding her activities, yet full of sweet endearments of her love for me.

8 August, 1820

Tuesday

Clementina and Mr Francis Sherbourne arrived just after Noon. She greeted me as if we had been parted for years. It was good to see her again. She was instantly sympathetic to Cordelia and offered to read to her while I took a *"well deserved"* rest.

Mr Sherbourne was kind enough to accompany me on a walk about the gardens. He was very flirtatious, but I had no heart for it. I see him with new eyes. He is still a very handsome gentleman, with his amazing green eyes, but they don't speak to me as Cole's do. I see now that what he presented was fascination, never love. I was so foolish, such a child before Cole's kiss placed him completely in my heart. No other man could share his sacred place.

We had a fine, if quiet dinner, and Mr Sherbourne's manner was all that was engaging but I know David saw the desperation in my eyes, for he took him off to play billiards after dinner and I was able to escape up to Cordelia's room where I spent the rest of the evening, giving my regrets to Clementina for ignoring her.

9 August, 1820

Wednesday

We have heard from Cousin Julian and Maddy. They will be staying in Newbury rather than descend upon us with Delia's injuries and our additional guests. I am sorry for this change in plans for it will deprive me of an opportunity to talk with her.

David, Clementina, Mr Sherbourne and I took a long walk today at mother's insistence I left Delia to her tender care. We were picking bilberries. I was paired with Mr Sherbourne because Clementina is obviously amusing herself with David, and he with her. Mr Sherbourne forbore to flirt ostentatiously with me which made me much easier in my mind.

It was rather soothing to have a man show such kind attentions to me when my heart is missing my dearest love. I don't know how we became so separated from David and Clementina. My basket was full of berries and my fingers slightly stained. We were joking around Mr Sherbourne and I. Sharing a few between ourselves as we progressed back towards the edge of the copse.

Oh diary, it was the most horrible thing to happen.

After we returned from our walk, I changed from my clothes

and told Molly I had a headache. I refused to see anyone, not even to attend Delia.

Addendum

(WHAT HAPPENED WITH MR SHERBOURNE...)

While in the copse, he tripped and fell. He lay as if unconscious. I rolled him over and immediately tried to determine if he was alive. Yes, people do not die from tripping, but he was so still for so long that I put my head to listen to his heart. Suddenly I was rolled over and on the ground. Mr Sherbourne was kissing me. His hands were touching me all over. For a moment I could not move I was in such shock and then I began to pummel him with my fists. It was long, horrible minutes before he let me go.

Mr Sherbourne watched me with a narrow gaze and proceeded to smoothly apologise for his actions, explaining they were an aberration of his injury. I did not care, I simply wanted to be away from him. I dropped the basket and ran from him. He caught me before I could get too far and told me to have a care for my Reputation.

Oh diary, it was the most horrible thing to happen. I have been sullied by this beast in gentleman's clothing. No man but my beloved Cole should have ever touched me, kissed me. Will he still want me now that this man defiled me? I do not know what to do or if I should tell someone but who?

10 August 1820

Thursday

The ball I had looked forward to with such excitement was instead a nightmare which I will never forget no matter how I try. Everything was so beautiful but the ugliness staining my heart could not appreciate it.

The Countess and her family greeting our family with the utmost graciousness. Mama and Papa were very pleased with these signs of goodwill. I was so very pleased to see Maddy. I wanted to talk to her so desperately, but I had not a chance to speak to her but for minutes at a time. Cousin Julian was there, for which I will have everlasting gratitude. He was gentle and kind and attentive and took me to supper.

I was forced to dance two dances with Mr Sherbourne for I could not betray his behaviour to the world without exposing my shame. He received only country dances from me, and I was careful to avoid his touch whenever possible, and yet he watched me so much of the time it frightens me. Oh, how I wish Cole was here. My soul aches for his comfort.

It was at least three of the clock before we left. Julian was still trying to find Maddy in the crush when we left.

Mr Sherbourne leaves tomorrow, early blessedly, and I have told Molly I will be sleeping in late and not to wake me for any reason. I will accept mother's condemnation and chastisement for my rude behaviour gladly rather than see him again. I do not know how I will suffer his sister's confiding presence in the meantime nor his return for her when the time comes.

11 August, 1820

Friday

This morning, I stayed in my bed late until Molly, at my directive, told me he was gone. I stayed in bed another hour to make sure my defection from his farewells were not noticeable. When I went downstairs, Mother was in a wild state. David had taken Clementina for a walk, or I do not think mother would have confessed the truth to me.

Maddy has Eloped! She and her lieutenant have gone to Gretna Green. They left quite early in the night, though no one appears to have noticed. The subterfuge turns out to rest upon her maid who changed into her costume mid celebration. The girl has been sacked of course but it appears that their flight has been well planned. Julian is racing to the border to try to turn them around, but the fact that Maddy left her family and is now alone with a man not a relative will ruin her more surely than this clandestine marriage. Therefore, it appears she will have to marry him simply to retrieve her reputation if never her status.

Another express came later with more details. Maddy's maid disappeared, and it appears with several trunks of Maddy's clothes.

There was a bitter irony to my aunt's comment that this act has been done with such military precision planning.

Mother is devastated by this blight on the family reputation but is only grateful the girl was not in her house when it happened. She asked me most closely about any information I might have had regarding this event. I prevaricated on this, for I did not feel comfortable betraying the extent of my cousin's confidences. I did admit that Maddy had confided her affections for this man, but did not tell of Annie's duties which included carrying secret correspondence between them. What use would it be now?

12 August, 1820

Saturday

Poor Clementina is not having a joyful visit. We naturally have not exposed our family's problem with her therefore she does not understand the tension which exists in our household. David and I do our best to entertain her. Harry has been coming over quite frequently too and he helps. We ride, we walk, she and I practice our music.

All my free time is split between tending Delia and the household. Mother is quite distraught with each express she receives.

I do not know why Aunt Acherton feels compelled to forward each titbit of information as it comes to them. Julian has been racing to catch up with them, but is miles behind them at every stop. Maddy has paid at every stop which is to prove she is complicit in this act so that her lieutenant cannot be said to have forced this upon her.

Their path has been sufficiently erratic that Julian's attempts to send a fast rider ahead to stop the next stage of horses has failed entirely. They have had no stops on their way, not to sleep or eat. All has been provided for them in baskets at stops along with their fresh horses. If they continue at this gruelling pace, they will reach the border sometime tomorrow.

I fear I will never again be allowed to see my cousin or to speak with her. It pains me to know that she will be cast off by her family. But Aunt has made it quite clear at this point that she will be. Though perhaps Julian does not yet realise it, his purpose is now only to see that she is married and then he will have no more purpose regarding Maddy remaining in his parents' eyes.

13 August, 1820

Sunday

We went to church and listened to a sermon on obeying our parents. A theme which has been drummed into my head in the last two days with fearsome ferocity.

I had a dreadful megrim by the time we left and mother seeing my paleness sent me to bed with a tisane. I slept for hours and when I woke, went to tend Delia who is doing much better. Her leg is healing well the doctor says and her crotchety nature has been ameliorated by Clementina's amusing games. Yes, she has been most helpful the last couple days in keeping Delia quiet and content. Clementina is a good and kind girl and despite her dreadful relative I find I still like her very well. We talk often, and though I do my best not to discuss her brother, she still mentions him with uncommon frequency. It is to be expected, no doubt but it pains me to hear the topic.

No word was had today on the matter of Maddy.

14 August, 1820

Monday

News has been received. The reason for Maddy's sudden flight was her lieutenant received his captaincy, but it was for a Regiment bound for Canada. They are even now on their way to the ship which will transport them to the Americas.

I cannot but wonder what she will make of the wilds she will find there. Deprivation and primitive conditions will be her constant companions, I am told. She has spent much of her money on their flight to Gretna. How much does she take as a dowry? Some pittance saved from her allowances, she is not one for saving, her jewels, gifts from her parents, sold. It is a shame.

I shall never see her again.

Again, I am selfishly saddened by my loss, even more than hers. I wish to be a better person, but fear I am a failure indeed.

15 August, 1820

Tuesday

I received a letter from Maddy. Mama did not see it which is a blessing. I know Mother would think it wrong for me to maintain a correspondence with her, but Maddy begs it of me, and I do not see how I can refuse her such a small thing. What harm can there be in keeping abreast of my cousin's life? Her disgrace cannot materially affect me through a letter. It cannot contaminate me as if a contagion will develop causing me to elope as well.

She has given me a place I may send a letter to her where her Husband, Captain Dennis Hammond will be stationed in Canada. I wrote a response immediately and struggled with how to get the letter to her. I do not want to bring Molly into this for it would be her position if we were caught. Finally, under strictest oath, I confided to David. He agreed that our correspondence though unapproved could do no harm and feels that if her parents had listened to her wishes with which she has patiently subscribed to for a year, then she would not have been driven to such desperate straits.

I did not expect to hear such a firm disapproval of our respected relatives handling of the situation. To see him actively frown upon their actions and if he did not give sanction to Maddy's actions there was at least tacit acceptance to them.

Therefore, my letter has been sent and should reach Maddy nearly as soon as she arrives upon those foreign shores. It soothes my mind to know that she will have one relative who has not forsaken her.

16 August, 1820

Wednesday

The household has fallen into a despondency. We do little but walk through the motions. Cordelia has returned to fretting. Wanting to be well and about. Clementina pines for excitement. David has gone to stay with friends. Mother appears quite unhappy with the entire Maddy affair. The news has come out and now even our neighbours know of the scandal, they talk behind our backs in whispers.

Papa has gone to Scotland for Grouse shooting and there is little to do but practice my music.

The weather is rainy and miserable here.

17 August, 1820

Thursday

Sally again has brought herself to my attention. She is the laziest creature imaginable. She was found sleeping in a spare bedroom rather than cleaning it. I spoke to Mrs Girling and she to Mother. It is agreed Sally's service will be terminated at Michaelmas.

I had a Letter from my cousin, Lady Felicia. She thinks she is with child, though she admits it is too soon to be sure. She had to share her news, and I am honoured by her confidence.

The kitten escaped Cordelia's room and found her way into Papa's. His favourite slippers have been massacred. Mother nearly had the kitten sent back to the barn, but Delia's pitiful pleading swayed her to let it remain.

The day was better than yesterday, the sun took time to peek from behind the clouds. Therefore, we had an impromptu lunch on the lawn. The footmen carried Delia out and she was delighted to be in the sun, even swaddled in enough rugs to keep her warm by Mother's standards.

18 August, 1820

Friday

Clementina and I went riding with Harry and Adam Buckman-Smythe. They were very glad to escape their lessons for a pleasant hour.

We had tea at the vicarage, and I was overjoyed to hear of Cole's continuing good health. I carefully expressed my good wishes for his continued health and success. I can but hope these words will be returned to him. We were then escorted back home by two boys much too energetic for we two girls.

Mother has banned novel reading for the time being. She apparently blames them for Maddy's misbehaviour. Instead, we must read improving works. Hannah More is a top choice. But other improving works fall not much short of it. The Bible of course is her preference, but even she cannot expect us only to read passages from the Bible. Clementina pointed out, to me, the Songs of Solomon and their often warm sentiments. So now we happily read the Bible under Mother's approving eye all the while we are striving to keep a solemn mien.

"Let him kiss me with the kisses of his mouth: for thy love is better

than wine." I cherish these words which so reflect my feelings for Cole. How I wish he could be here at my side.

My dreams are troubled with him. Pleasant though they are I cannot get enough of their sweet nectar.

19 August, 1820

Saturday

Rain and lightning kept us within the entire day.

Everyone was quite snappish with each other. Delia refuses to stay in her room another moment. She wishes to hear no more of improving tracts. Clementina and I were quite in agreement with her, so we did nothing to soothe her temper and finally Mama gave in and let us re-read Ms Austen's Persuasion to her. I must assume she intends it to be a morality lesson in that waiting upon the approval of family and friends is better than reckless disregard for family. I am not sure I take the same message to heart.

Dinner was burnt and mother quite displeased. She had me attend her when she took Cook to task. Cook was not best pleased to have an audience during her dressing down.

20 August, 1820

Sunday

Weather continues horribly. No one wishes to be about. Clementina had a megrim that kept her in bed.

Mama insisted I rise and practice the pianoforte. She came in to listen while attending to mending and told me I was not practising enough if I was making so many errors. So now I must practice two hours a day.

Afterwards she had me join her in mending and other stitchery. She was pleased to compliment my fine stitches. It was good to have something for which she was proud. She has been very hard to please of late.

David returned after dinner. Mama was delighted to see him as tomorrow is his birthday. She nearly fell upon his neck to greet him.

21 August, 1820

Monday

It was a quiet celebration for David's 20th birthday. He was pleased with the handkerchiefs from both Maddy (who had left them with me) and myself. Though Papa was not there, he had sent along a new saddle for him. Mama had boots made up by his favourite bootmaker as well as some other small tokens which pleased David mightily.

I am delighted to have David back home. He and I and Clementina went for a ride. His pleasure in the new saddle is inestimable.

David was unhappy to hear that Sally would be terminated at Michaelmas, but seemed to finally understand it had nothing to do with what happened between them but rather her inability to do the work she was hired to do.

We had a plethora of special confections made by Cook for David's enjoyment. The Cook always has liked him best of all of us. Mama could not stop watching him the entire meal. It is a truth that she loves her firstborn son best of all.

22 August, 1820

Tuesday

We had a letter from Sammy. He will be returning to us in a few more days, to be with us before he returns to school. David has offered to retrieve him from our Uncle's and mother has agreed, though reluctantly.

Delia spends most of the day downstairs now with the footman carrying her from room to room. She is becoming quite spoiled by her injury. There is no small attention to be missed on her behalf.

Clementina, David, Harry and I rode out for a long time which was very pleasant. Clementina quite likes to be the centre of attention and strove to have both Harry and David flirting with her. Harry simply blushed and dropped back to ride beside me as much as possible. Poor man was most flustered.

A light shower caught us just as we were within sight of the house. Mother immediately sent us up to our rooms to change for fear of contracting a cold. Harry was forced to make do with our hospitality as the rain drenched the ground. He made do with a jacket of David's which was both too long and too tight for him, but he took it in good stead and kept me company while I practised the piano. David and Clementina sketched while mother complacently embroidered by the fire where Delia was sulkily doing the same on a sampler.

The rain lasted a long hour and by the time it stopped, Harry's jacket was dry, and he was able to ride home in good form. Mama sent an invitation with him to dinner for the Vicar and wife as well as Harry. We will look forward to the extra entertainment.

Forty-three years later...

10th May, 1863

Sunday

My birthday. I am old. I have been old for some time, but today I feel it most keenly. I have been on this earth for 60 years. Birthdays are for the young. However, I summoned my happiest thoughts and brightest smile for dinner - held in my honour. I ignored the aches in my bones and pretended to the guests who gathered this night and showered me with presents and kisses that I am the happiest of women.

One of my birthday presents sent to me was this diary. I must admit it was a surprise to receive it from David. I have not had a diary since I was a girl, before I married my darling Cole. After marriage I was too busy to keep a journal, but now I have the time, though what I shall write in it I do not know for my life is not as exciting as it once.

None of my children were here for my birthday, nor my siblings, and of course the greatest hole in my life, Cole, is absent from my side. It is unbearable to celebrate any festivity without him beside me, but I continue to try.

When he retired from his duties for the government, and we left London for the peacefulness of this little village, near Whitby on the North Yorkshire coast I expected years ahead of us enjoying life together. It was not to be, dear diary. But I am thankful for the blessed marriage we shared full of love and happiness. Cole got to see his three children married and held his grandchildren before he suddenly departed this life.

Birthdays always remind me of those who are no longer with me. Cole, my parents, (Papa's teasing smile and Mama's gentle touch,) and aunts and uncles long gone, along with the old family house in Berkshire where I grew up. David inherited it once our parents passed away but sold it. He said the memories were too sad to make him want to live there.

This morning Mr Perkins (my gardener) gave me a posy of tulips from the garden and a gracious bow as I was inspecting the new rose just coming into bud. I felt like a young maid once more - at least for a little while.

I miss *my love*. How well he used to celebrate my birthdays. What is the day without him?

May 11th, 1863

Monday

I am a little tired due to the late festivities of the previous night.

However, I gained much joy from having my dearest friends for dinner. The children all sent me letters and my eldest Oliver, his wife Fran, and my grandsons will be here soon so spend some time with me. I am a fortunate woman indeed.

I have started to search for a new tapestry to replace the one in the library. I shall be sorry to see it taken down, for it was my sister-in-law's work and given to me as a new bride. But smoke from the fireplace has ruined it and it needs better stitching than my talents allow to reform it. I shall have it sent away to be mended but in the meantime, I will need something to replace it on the wall.

I dined at the vicarage this eve with dear friends, Reverend Jonas Tulridge and his charming wife Fanny, along with Mrs Folkstone, Miss Jenny Folkstone and Mr Bains, the former postmaster who befriended Cole and myself on the first day we docked from the steamer in Whitby bay. Jonas won at cards. Next time I shall have to be sharper as he does enjoy triumphing over me.

A cool day. Storm clouds brewing.

May 12th, 1863

Tuesday

Storms blew wild all the previous night, made quite a mess in the garden, luckily the orchard blossom has finished. The dove cote was blown down, but the birds are fine, though shaken, I'm sure. Perkins and his young lad had much to do to clean up the gardens and lawns. Any snapped flowers I brought into the house to arrange in vases so as not to waste them.

Ships in the bay in Whitby were displaced but reports from the post carrier was that none were smashed against the rocks, which is a blessed outcome. Many were out at sea fishing.

As I look out my bedroom window now, so high on the clifftop, above the bay, the setting sun is rendering the sky golden, strips of windblown cloud look like an artist's turn of the brush. David would enjoy painting such a scene.

The clasp on my best brooch broke today, I am heartbroken, as it was a present from Cole for my 30th birthday. Mrs Clancy (housekeeper) assured me it can be easily mended by a jeweller in Whitby. I shall take it in and see what can be done about it.

May 13th, 1863

Wednesday

Received a letter from Cordelia, such joy it brings me. She is a grandmother again, a little girl called Alma Jane. My niece Mariana is weak after the birth, and I shall say extra prayers for both mother and baby's wellbeing.

I'm excited to see Oliver and the family and am impatient for the time to pass before they are here. I had the carpets taken out today in all the lower rooms. Then I ordered for the curtains and drapes to be washed. I must not let the house become tardy now that *my love* has gone - he would not be pleased.

I sometimes wander the rooms of this beautiful house and think I can hear him. I see a shadow and think he's there. Alas, he is not, and my heart is heavy.

Cole's solicitor and now mine, Mr Ramsgate came today with too many things for me to sign. Such paperwork and figures makes me weary. Two years after Cole's death and there is still much I must sign for and check accounts for, but I know it is for my own benefit. Cole provided well for this family and to keep such incomes I must play my part with signatures and taking an interest in Mr Ramsgate's information as he does keep it all going splendidly for me. Both our sons, Oliver and Jonathan, play an enormous part in keeping their father's businesses in profit. I am so proud of them.

Re-reading *Uncle Tom's Cabin*. The newspapers' reports of the Civil War in America show no signs of the carnage stopping.

Weather - The day cool.

May 14th, 1863

Thursday

Began indexing the library, it hasn't been done since we first moved here ten years ago, and *my love* and I have bought many more books since then. Touching *my love's* books made me feel closer to him on this dull, damp day.

Tomorrow I must venture into town for fittings. Two new day dresses, a new wider crinoline, (how the fashions change so quickly) three summer hats and a short cape. Such extravagance!

Bad news from across the Atlantic, America in turmoil, such battles they fight. I pray for that country's mothers.

Rain all day. Weather cool. I order fires to be lit again which vexed me greatly as the spring cleaning is in earnest.

May 15th, 1863

Friday

Very eventful day.

Spent most of the day in Whitby, so pleased that my excellent seamstress moved her business to our small sea-side port on her semi-retirement. What would I do without her?

After my fittings, I went to buy embroidery threads, extra needles, and cotton thread. I also dipped into Mr Blake's Books & Music Shoppe mainly to buy some new sheet piano music but against my better judgement bought two small books, one of poetry and another on plants & trees. I am so undisciplined.

One my way home, I called to see Mrs Chantrall, one of our tenants, her health is so uncertain after her tenth baby, but she rallied to see me, bless her. I gave her a basket of victuals.

I was glad to arrive home safely despite the horrid muddy roads. I tempted fate by journey out today with such threatening rain.

A letter was waiting for me from my friend, sweet Audrey, who is overseas in India. I still remember the day we met, not long after my wedding day and our move to Kensington in London.

Audrey's husband was a good friend of Cole's and Audrey and I became close as a result. I'm glad to read that she is well. I miss seeing her.

Weather cool and windy. Out to sea it looks frightful. Nightfall has come early with angry black storm clouds.

May 16th, 1863

Saturday

Busy all morning with visitors. I was impatient for them to go as I was eagerly awaiting the best of arrivals.

Then, at midday, they arrived. Oliver, Fran, and my grandsons, Albie, Arthur, and Frank.

How my darling boys have grown! Immediately they filled the house with noise and activity. Albie is the image of my dearest love, Arthur is so like his father in looks (more like me) and temperament while Frank is considered like Fran's father, the distinguished Robyn Morecombe.

After luncheon, which I was sure the boys would explode from overindulging, we walked the dogs along the clifftops. Even Blackie and Hollie found their youth again romping with my boys. Cole would have been so happy to see his old dogs running alongside his grandsons.

As I write, my boys are sleeping soundly in their shared bedroom, and my two furry constant companions are sprawled in front of my bedroom fire quite exhausted! Oliver and Fran are still downstairs reading before the fire. Fran looked pale on exiting the carriage today but rallied after our walk. Oliver reminds me so much of his father in manner and expressions, more so than his brother Jonathan who resembles David a great deal.

How I love to see them under my roof where I can care for them.

Weather windy.

May 17th, 1863

Sunday

Walked! Oh, my how I walked! But it pleases my boys to have me tag along behind them.

After church, where Jonas (Reverend Tulridge) gave a wonderful sermon on the effects of the American war and how we should look to God and each other for comfort when all we hear is such terrible tragedies, we had a picnic down by the shore.

Fran read while Oliver and I took the boys over the rocks with Blackie and Hollie following us. We filled the hamper with shells, rocks, and all manner of things, which did not please Mrs Higby (cook) when she saw it returned in such a state. She pretended to be severe but one shy smile from Arthur had her giving out plates of warm scones and steaming cups of hot chocolate. How I laughed.

In fact, I laughed so much today I felt guilty, but Oliver commented on how it suits me and my dreadful years of grieving. So, I shall endeavour to do more of it, I know *my love* would admire me. Cole once said my happy spirit was what first attracted me to him. He would have so enjoyed being by the water today with our little men.

The wind continues, but I hardly notice it.

May 18th, 1863

Monday

Fran and I cut roses to bring inside preventing the wind to do anymore damage. The sun shone brightly on us and even brought a little colour to our cheeks. Fran is shining with a secret delight, which I'm sure she will confide in me presently.

Oliver and the boys went with Mr Simons, the game keeper, to the neighbouring Lipton estate for a day of rabbit netting. Mr Simons has a pair of ferrets and a little terrier dog that is a great rabbit catcher. My neighbour and good friend, Don Lipton, greatly misses *my love* nearly as much as me, and having no sons of his own, delights in the company of Oliver and the boys. How grown up they looked with their guns hooked over their arms. Frank, at only 11, was quite overwhelmed.

Blackie limping - sore back leg. Too much romping with the boys I believe. She doesn't acknowledge her age.

A letter from Delia. Mariana is not recovering from the birth and the baby is weak. The doctor visits them daily. I do worry for them both.

Weather warmer and wind has disappeared.

May 19th, 1863

Tuesday

Oliver took Fran and the boys down to Whitby for the day, giving me some much-needed rest. How the boys bound about me, always asking my opinion and wanting me to look at this and that. I adore them so can never say no - much to Oliver's disproval.

Today the library tapestry was rolled up and sent away to London to be mended. I caught up with my accounts and did much letter writing.

Fran still has not indulged her secret. Though I can guess it.

Received a letter from Maddy in Canada. She is well and writes of her charity work in the remote provinces of that large country. Her second husband is a minister, and they are both devoted to helping others. I think back to the days when my cousin came to stay with us in Berkshire and her subsequent elopement with her dashing lieutenant. Dennis Hammond died three years after they arrived in Canada and my uncle and aunt pleaded for Maddy to come home to England. She didn't. Instead, she became a companion for a rich old woman who left her all her money when she died. Maddy remarried, to a certain Mr Fulton and became a minister's wife. Something I could never have foreseen. Maddy's letters are sporadically sent for she is often away in far-flung places in the wilderness, but they are brimming with interesting news when they do arrive.

A letter from David. His latest collection of art was well-received at the opening of his exhibition in London. I do worry about him. His health has been testing of late.

I pray it doesn't rain while the boys are here. I doubt my house could stand too much indoor activity. Should it rain, I'll send them down to the kitchen to Mrs Higby. I'm sure she'll find something to occupy their busy minds and fingers.

Weather - warming.

May 20th, 1863

Wednesday

Many letters arrived today. One each from David, Clementina, and Cousin Ned, Cousin Felicia in Australia, as well as one from Harry. Harry is looking to retire from his doctoring. Felicia writes one of her children, Josiah and his family, are moving to New South Wales (Felicia lives in Melbourne - a good distance from there). Josiah will be within 50 miles of my brother Sammy's property.

Arthur wrote me a beautiful poem today, remembering his darling Grandfather. I had to quickly escape him to cry alone, so wondrous it was.

Mrs Folkstone and Jenny came for morning tea.

Later, I took the boys back down to the shore. It was very warm today suddenly. The boys got awfully wet. Fran was most displeased, yet how can I say no to my little men?

Frank is so adventurous with Albie keen to lead the way. Arthur took my arm, and we walked and talked. He is so clever and astute.

I never want them to leave and told Oliver them same. Alas, he informs me they must go in two days' time. The boys must return to school but shall return again for the summer.

Blackie still limps though not as bad.

Inspected the orchard today, there should be an abundance of fruit come harvest time. Apples, pears, apricots, and plums all showing such promise of a bountiful haul. Mr Perkins is netting the trees for the birds are keen to deplete us of our fruit.

Don Lipton came to dinner.

Weather - sunny.

May 21st, 1863

Thursday

Fran helped me with embroidering a large piece of work which I've decided will be framed and hung over the fireplace in the library until the tapestry is mended and returned. What beautiful work she does, so proficient.

We've had a cool day today after such early warmth. I set the boys a task of counting the pigeons in the pigeon loft. Then Albie, always so heroic, ventured to catch four for dinner. I'm not sure Mrs Higby was pleased or not by this sudden alteration to her menu.

Mrs Nell Watts called. A dear woman, a widow like me and lives in the hamlet at the southern end of my estate. Her son is a doctor, and he is leaving for new pastures, her words not mine, she is going with him. Cornwall apparently. So, she is giving up her home and him the practice in the hamlet, which means the nearest doctor will be in Whitby some five miles from here.

Government work has called Oliver home to London, and sadly the boys must return to boarding school, but Fran is staying here with me longer, which I am eternally grateful for. I can never reveal to them how lonely I become some days. They leave the day after tomorrow.

Oliver tells us that once he's sorted his business problems, he'll be back, but Fran is worried he'll not take care of himself while he's away. She does fuss so. However, she confided in me her secret, and as I expected she is with child. She hopes this long period (11 years) since Frank's birth will result in a girl child, but that is in the hands of fate I tell her.

Got a missive today from David, his health is not good at the moment, and he wishes to visit me and my fresh sea breezes. Of course I told him to come immediately, London in the summer months is appalling.

I will make sure his stay here will lengthen past summer. He's alone and so am I, we should spend our last years together.

Weather - fair.

May 22nd, 1863

Friday

The weather changed overnight and kept us indoors. The boys made a stage and put on a show for Fran and I and even asked the servants to attend. They did a wonderful show and had us all laughing. Arthur tried to stay serious but, in the end, laughed as hard as the rest of us as Frank and Albie were such a comedy act.

David sent a telegram and arrives tomorrow, glory be to God. He will take the overnight train. On receiving his missive, I ordered for the room he always uses to be aired and made ready.

The boys went fishing yet again. We shall have fish dinners for days to come I'm afraid.

Fran and I have begun to knit and sew for the new addition.

Weather cool.

May 23rd, 1863

Saturday

Most distressful news. Delia's new granddaughter was taken from this earth the night before last. All is distraught. How my poor niece, Mariana must be suffering. I sent a letter to her straightaway and had my coachman take it into Whitby to be posted within the hour of receiving Delia's letter.

David sent a message that he shall be arriving late tomorrow now, as his journey has been fraught with problems. What they are he did not say.

We said a sad goodbye to Oliver and the boys. Fran held back her tears bravely, for the boys will not return to her again for many weeks, until the school term is complete. I shall miss my little men.

Blackie and Hollie moan from lack of attention, so used to their companions now.

Weather - warming with a strong breeze.

May 24th, 1863

Sunday

At long last my darling David is here with me. My brother arrived minutes after we return home from church. He had a terrible journey north with train delays and long stoppages. He is pale and thin, but under my tender care and Mrs Higby's delicious temptations he shall be hale and hearty soon. I am most pleased he is here. He does not look after himself in London.

Received a letter from my darling daughter Catherine. She, Charles and Josephina arrived safely in France and are enjoying the sights. I do hope they remain safe and well. My granddaughter, Josephina is a delight to me and Cole used to say that she is my image in every way.

I wrote to Harry telling him of the vacancy of a doctor in the hamlet. He is close to retiring from his own practice and this move might be of some benefit to him. He often tells me when he visits here how much he enjoys being in this area. Whitby has many attractions and the countryside around the coast is rather pretty for walks and carriage rides. I do hope he considers the opportunity. I confess I would like to have such another dear friend close to me.

Weather - a drift of rain today - cloudy again.

May 25th, 1863

Monday

Posted mail today. Another letter to Delia, and one to poor Mariana, bless her grieving soul.

Mrs Fanny Tulridge, Miss Enid Kitsen, (who has a fondness for David) Mrs Folkstone and Miss Jenny Folkstone called for afternoon tea. They have met Fran previously, and we made a nice party sitting on the terrace overlooking the gardens. Mrs Folkstone was widowed at a young age and brought her daughter up alone. Her husband had a fleet of fishing trawlers which Mrs Folkstone sold off some years ago. They live a quiet life in a cottage in Whitby. I do like the two ladies very much. Mrs Folkstone is my age and desperate for Jenny to be married but at forty years old, it seems Jenny is fated to remain a spinster.

Mrs Clancey had the two maids turning out the bedrooms after the boys left. Under their beds the maids found an assortment of little treasures, shells, drawings, balls, an old bird's nest, smooth rocks and dog-eared books. I told them to put all of it into baskets and leave them at the foot of the beds. The boys will enjoy visiting their riches when they return.

David is not rallying as he should, and I wrote again to Harry for his advice.

Unfortunately, David's health hasn't been good for some years.

Previously, when David has succumbed to one of his bad bouts of illness, Harry has examined him and believes David has some wasting disease. He suspects that David continues to suffer a reoccurrence of a past tropical ailment. Which of course could be correct since David spent a few years in Asia and Africa.

I am very frightened that this illness has returned to David once more, but am determined to nurse him forever if need be.

Fran is again sick in the mornings. I advised her to stay in bed today as the weather has turned sour. When will summer make an appearance?

May 26th, 1863

Tuesday

A quiet day at home.

David is a little better but not greatly improved. He does have some colour and is moving around the house a little. He's so awfully thin, not like him at all. I have sent a note to Don Lipton to tell him of David's arrival, for I know they have had such good conversations in the past and seeing Don might give David someone else to converse with. Although David is sleeping a great deal. I pray that will soon have him sorted back to health.

I have Mrs Clancey seeing to everything in the house and turning away callers, for I am too busy caring for David and Fran is also rather peaky and tired.

Mr Roberts, the estate manager, wanted a moment of my time regarding some boundary stonewalls but I simply told him to do what he saw fit about it. If men are needed to be hired to repair the broken walls, then it should be done. He spoke of our prized ram being lame and his administrations to address the problem. I felt terrible for being impatient with him and his concerns, but I had much to do with caring for my brother and daughter-in-law. I shall venture to the estate's home farm tomorrow and speak with him more in-depth about the farm's problems.

I've requested Mrs Higby to cook some plain foods but wholesome and filling dishes which will do both David and Fran the world of good.

Wrote to Felicia and Catherine.

Weather – a bright and sunny day.

May 27th, 1863

Wednesday

The day was fine without any breeze, and we ventured to hold a picnic on in the gardens this afternoon when Don Lipton arrived. David look much more himself, and ate heartily if only for my sake, poor lamb. He had some colour and slept for an hour in the warm sun and felt very refreshed afterwards.

A letter arrived from darling Josephina in Paris. She writes so well and was full of wonders of Paris. How I envy her youth and vigour of fourteen years. She is seeing Paris early in her life, but the images will sear in her mind forever more. I would so love to be there and watch the city unfold its glory before her eyes and watch the expressions fly across her beautiful face.

Harry replied to my letter with a keen interest to move to the hamlet. He is preparing to visit us and shall be here in three days' time. I am excited to see my very good friend again. His yearly visits are always something I look forward to.

Delia writes that she is in great anguish as Mariana's health is declining. Oh, what terrible news it is to hear. I pray to God she recovers.

Weather - warm but overcast.

May 28th, 1863

Thursday

David felt well enough to walk along the clifftops. Fran and I joined him. The gulls wheeled and cried today making me feel sad with their sorrowful sound.

David squeezed my arm and told me tales of our childhood. Soon we were both wanting to be riding our horses like days of old. We fondly remembered Nutmeg and Coriander. I haven't ridden for some years, preferring to be taken in the carriage or drive the gig now. The roads into Whitby are steep and I am not young (or silly) enough anymore to try my hand at such reckless pursuits such a cantering along clifftops. David told me he hadn't ridden for over a year. And I feel that now he couldn't hold his stirrup even if he so wished.

Why do we grow old and frail I ask? Our minds stay whole, yet our bodies betray us so terribly.

With David feeling more his old self, I decided to hold a dinner party to celebrate Harry's arrival. I shall invite other friends to dinner. Reverend Jonas and Fanny Tulridge, Mrs Folkstone, and Jenny, Don Lipton, Mr Jem Kilmore and his wife Regina from Whitby and Mr Walt Kitsen and his sister Enid Kitsen from a neighbouring estate, all people Cole and I met and became friends with when we first moved to North Yorkshire.

I must get some sleep for I have much to prepare in the morning.

Weather - fair.

May 29th, 1863

Friday

I was pleasantly surprised this morning, after I had finished writing out my invitations for the dinner party and answering my correspondence, I walked into the conservatory to find David painting. As far as I know he hadn't picked up a brush for many a month. Once he had finished his collection for the exhibition he had exhausted himself. It did my heart a great deal of good to see him painting again.

Received a short letter from Delia, Mariana is desperately ill, and I shudder to think what will happen if she doesn't recover. David and I shall both pray for her. This news has disheartened David considerably. He feels a young mother should not be taken when he, an old man, should be left behind. Of course, I tell him this is nonsense, but he will not listen to me.

We were surprised to see Oliver arrive in the later afternoon. He'd taken the night train from London to York and the coach from York to Whitby. He came with no announcement but brought such happiness. Fran was beside herself to have him with her again.

And another surprise, Oliver mentions he saw Jonathan in

Town. My second son will be visiting next month I am told. What joy that will bring me. Jonathan has been in the West Indies for over a year and only returned this week. He send his regards to us all but business keeps him in London.

I spent a good hour with Mrs Higby to make sure the dinner party menu was perfect, and she was purchasing everything that she needed. Mrs Clancey and the maids made up the Blue room for Harry's stay.

Weather - fair.

May 30th, 1863

Saturday

Dearest Harry arrived safely. The coach dropped him at my door at half past the hour of 1 in the afternoon. He was tired from the journey from Berkshire but relieved to see me I could tell. Always a quiet man, he has, over the long years of our friendship, been such a mainstay in my life, and David's, of course. The two men warmly greeted each other like brothers.

Mrs Clancey showed Harry up to his room so he could wash and change before he joined us for luncheon. Age has widened Harry's shoulders, and greyed his hair and he wears glasses to read, but his kind eyes still are the same and his smile warmed my heart.

After luncheon I left David and Harry to talk in confidence about Harry's health. Fran and Oliver went into Whitby and I walked to the estate's home farm to check on the ram's progress. Mr Roberts was pleased with how the ram was recovering. We spoke of general farm issues, the ploughing, sowing, and rotations of crops, all matters I've had to learn quickly since Cole's passing. However, I am no farmer, and I leave all judgement to Mr Roberts. Cole trusted the man to run the estate, and I continued to do so.

On my walk back to the house I passed Mr Simons, the game keeper, who held up a brace of cock pheasants, which would in the near future grace my dining table.

Weather - sunny.

May 31st, 1863

Sunday

After church, David felt a little off, so we stayed indoors as the wind came up most cool. The sea breezes can be bracing no matter what time of the year.

I wrote to Delia, sending my prayers to her and Mariana. How my dear sister must be suffering, and having no one to share her responsibilities and fears, for everyone knows, to our eternal shame, that the man she married was never very good in supporting her. I ridicule myself for staying silent all these years, but I know I cannot tread into her marriage. Still, David and I am united in that Delia, when the crisis is over, must come stay with us for a timely rest, and not bring her useless husband with her.

A kitchen maid spilled boiling water over herself this morning, once more I had to call on dear Harry. Luckily the girl's skirts prevented major damage to her legs.

A letter from Jonathan telling me he should be arriving within a few weeks. I long to see him.

At long last I received a letter from my brother Sammy in Australia where he has lived for over a decade. But his news was tragic. His wife Julia died some months ago. The distressing announcement was met with gasps when I read it to the others. We had never met Julia, for Sammy married her in Australia and they'd never travelled to England. We are all in deepest sorrow for our beloved Sammy. Losing your life partner is a pain that cuts deep.

I mentioned whether I should cancel the dinner party, but David convinced me to go ahead with it. A quiet dinner with friends cannot be seen as disrespectful when the incident happened many months ago.

Weather – sunny with a cool breeze.

June 1st, 1863

Monday

My dinner party succeeded better than I hoped. Mrs Higby excelled in her dishes making me proud.

David sparkled as usual when in company of the fairer sex. His early sadness about Sammy all but gone.

When our guests had departed, I noticed the tired line around David's mouth and insisted he go to bed immediately. I do so fear about his health.

Miss Enid Kitsen, I'm sure, still felt a stirring in her breast at the sight of my elder brother, for she didn't mask her excited expression as quickly as she should on first arriving and seeing him. Poor woman. To be thwarted in love can be so tiresome. Despite meeting David only a small number of times when he visited in previous years, Enid had set her sights on my brother and not distance nor time could persuade her otherwise. Naturally, David flirted with her outrageously, not helping the matter, but I know he has no intentions of ever marrying.

The newspapers are full of the sorry news over the Atlantic. The Confederates win one battle only for the Unionists to win the next.

The Māori in New Zealand still continue to rebel, as do the Poles against Russia. Has the whole world gone mad?

No news from Delia.

Weather - fair.

June 2nd, 1863

Tuesday

Feeling a little unwell today, my head aches and I have a slight temperature. Harry examined me and believes I have caught some ailment of the chest.

I've spent the day reading and sewing in my room, so David does not get it too, for he must not get something else on top of the illness he is recovering from. Harry has banished both David and Fran from my room so they don't become afflicted. However, he and Oliver visited almost every hour to keep me company.

Blackie and Hollie have stayed with me, sharing my bad humour, such faithfulness is hard to come by.

Weather - hot

June 3rd, 1863

Wednesday

Another day spent in bed, but feeling better. David insisted on visiting me, silly man.

Was so very pleased when he brought the mail to me. I received a letter from Audrey. My dearest friend writes that she is coming home from India, Reggie is retiring at last. Audrey writes they will settle in North Yorkshire, within a day's ride from Whitby because they have enjoyed this area when visiting Cole and me previously. I'm so happy I'm beside myself.

Blackie has a swollen eye. David saw a grass seed was imbedded in it and removed it successfully.

Harry has declared he will move to the hamlet and make use of the cottage and dispensary there to set up his doctoring practice. I am most pleased to have him so near. He has spent the day organising for the purchase of the cottage and the necessary paperwork and advertisements of his intentions in the Whitby newspaper.

It has been a day of happy news indeed.

Weather - warm and sunny.

June 4th, 1863

Thursday

Feeling better today and left my bedroom. Oliver left for London as the boys have finished school. He will send them by train to York and I shall have my carriage waiting for them at the train station. Oliver is to stay in London for a short time to see to his business affairs.

Miss Enid Kitsen called for tea this morning, and stayed over an hour talking to David, much to my amusement. Normally the woman is gone within twenty minutes.

Later, David and Harry went fishing this afternoon, and David came back with colour in his cheeks. He believes himself to be indestructible, only I know his is not.

Delia writes of her pain. Baby Alma's loss is so terribly hard for them all, especially dear Mariana, who fights bravely, but Delia informs me the situation is lost, and the vicar has been called to her bedside. How will Mariana's husband and children cope without her? My niece is such a sweet young woman, so like Delia and it saddens me greatly that God calls her to Him.

Roses are looking glorious in the garden. I have many vases filled with them in the house. Their scent comforts me.

Wrote a good many letters and updated my account ledger. Weather - warm.

June 5th, 1863

Friday

The most distressing news today. Mariana has left us during the night with her family by her side. The telegram I received from Ian (Delia's husband) this morning filled my heart with complete sorrow. Three motherless children must now look towards their father, Hamish, and grandmother Delia for their support. Hamish's elderly parents live in Scotland can be of no assistance due to their age.

I went into Whitby and telegraphed Oliver to alert him to the news. I have written to Jonathan and Catherine though I do not expect Catherine to travel back from France for the funeral and told her so, since she wouldn't make it in time and must continue her visit for Josephina's sake. I do understand that Catherine will be grieved at this news, for she and Mariana were close.

I shall make the journey in a few days to Berkshire for the funeral. Harry will accompany me as he must return home to pack up his house and affairs there.

Blackie's eye better.

The west wall shrubbery is bursting with buds as the garden is blooming in this warm weather. The garden is such a soothing place. It brings me so much joy to walk amongst such glorious flowers. Mr Perkins and his boy are extremely busy tending to the gardens and the house kitchen garden. We have a good amount of produce all ready for Mrs Higby.

Weather - warm.

June 6th, 1863

Saturday

I am completely better today, though down in spirits. The sun shone beautifully and David, Harry and I went for a drive to clear our heads. Mariana played heavily on our thoughts.

On arriving home, I received another letter from Sammy. He must have written his letters close together, though with the distance of a half a world between us, who can tell how long ships take to bring loved ones' letters to us. There are so many things that can delay such voyages.

I was happy to hear from him. He writes he is very busy on his property. But I detected a loneliness within his words. Julia died leaving him without issue, and I believe he feels it keenly. He is alone, away from family with only farmhands and servants to keep him company. I shall write him tomorrow.

The first flower of a cross propagation of my red and white begonias have resulted in a pale pink blush colour. I am most satisfied, though I'm of the opinion that Mr Perkins isn't so.

Don Lipton called later this afternoon to sup with us.

I have much to do tomorrow to prepare to travel to Berkshire on Monday. The funeral is set for Tuesday. Fran will stay here as the boys are due to arrive here on Monday.

Weather – warm with a slight sea breeze.

June 7th, 1863

Sunday

Rain tumbled down today keeping us indoors after church. David had wished to fish, but on no account would I let him. Silly man, he's like a child I must constantly watch.

I was pleased to put him to more industrious work. He wrote to Sammy, he cleaned his shooting gun, and then later we played chess by the fire while Harry read, and Fran played solitaire.

Blackie is ageing, like us all, and it saddens me so to see it.

Weather – rain – the garden needs it.

June 15th, 1863

Monday

Oh, diary it has been a week since I have written in your fine pages. I forgot to take you with me to Berkshire.

What a dreadful week it was. Such pain to witness as Mariana's coffin was placed into the ground. My poor sister was in pieces, I did my best to aid her, but her disagreeable husband was forever in my way with his uselessness and disparaging remarks. I cannot stand the man's presence!

Mariana's husband was inconsolable in his grief. The children bewildered by the loss of their mother.

I made Delia promise me she will come to me for a rest when she felt able to travel. I invited Hamish and the children as well, but I am not sure whether he will accept the invitation.

So much post waited my return, but more importantly my grandsons were here to embrace me with much needed warmth and familiarity. How I can never take them for granted, my dear little men. I'm sure they have grown!

I received another short letter from Audrey, she breaks her journey home at Nice. She writes to request me to look for suitable housing for her and Reggie. The original house they had chosen to rent has been withdrawn from that state and sold instead. I will do my best for her.

It is good to be home.

Weather - fine.

June 16th, 1863

Tuesday

David was ill all day. I kept him in bed as he has developed a cough. I blame the travelling to Berkshire and mingling with strangers at the funeral.

I was kept busy with household affairs for most of the day. Mrs Clancey hurt her arm lifting a heavy box up in the attics.

Paid many bills.

The boys wanted my attention, and I promised to give it to them tomorrow once I have everything sorted within the house.

Blackie is refusing to eat. I am most fearful.

Weather – rain storms.

June 17th, 1863

Wednesday

David stayed late in bed this morning while I visited an acquaintance.

Old Mrs Reed (former Housekeeper now living in a cottage on estate) asked me to read her letter from her son, Jim, who lives in Spain. Her eyesight is nearly gone now, poor dear. She was delighted to hear of him settled and healthy. His wife was safely delivered of their eighth child, a boy. They are living in a small port where he works on repairing boats. He writes of days in the hot sun and his children growing like beans.

On my return home, David was up and sitting in the drawing room tutoring the boys on drawing techniques. Rain began after luncheon. Fran was most displeased by it for the boys are restless kept inside.

Received a telegram this morning. Delia is coming to stay with Mariana's children as to give them a time away from a house filled with grief. Also, their father Hamish is to return to his regiment, the 47th Highland Regulars. I'm sure he is allowed more time, yet I believe he wishes to immerse himself back into something familiar, and away from what he has lost. Poor Mariana.

So, David and I will soon have six children to fuss and spoil. Our three little men and Mariana's three sweet little ones. I just hope Delia brings enough nursemaids, for it's been a long time since I had the use of one.

Lord this quiet old house shan't know what has hit it! But I shall enjoy having Delia here, it's been over six months since she visited me and only the Lord knows how much she needs a rest. Her telegram mention no word of her husband joining her, for which I am thankful.

Blackie still not eating.

Weather – rain easing.

June 18th, 1863

Thursday

David was well enough to accompany me, and we spent the day driving the local district, looking at houses to let for Audrey and Reggie. We saw four in total today – all within an hour's drive of my estate. One, Cherry Tree Cottage was particularly pleasing, and I would be most happy to show it to Audrey and Reggie as a future home for them. The house came with five acres of land, a pretty garden, a water well and a solid roof. I saw no dampness or leaks on my inspection. On three sides the boundary was boarded by woodland.

Of course, it is their choice. I do hope I can find her something suitable within a half day journey, so we can visit each other more easily. I become more selfish the older I get it seems.

Blackie won't leave her bed. I fear her time is coming to an end and I am broken-hearted. She was Cole's favorite.

Weather - warm.

June 19th, 1863

Friday

I am afraid to report that I was at sixes and sevens this day. I had Mrs Clancey and the maids running about like mindless things this morning as we prepare the rooms for Delia and the children's arrival tomorrow.

Fran is sickly with the child. She seems to become paler each day as her stomach grows. I wish Harry was here to attend to her. I have written to him for advice. The boys are wearing on her nerves. They were simply dreadful in behaviour today as the storm clouds kept them indoors.

Finally, they made even *me* raise my voice to them! Their faces! I dispatched them up to the attics with scrubbing brushes! That'll teach them to think their old Grandmother is easily foxed. I wish the sun would shine again if only to send the boys outside. David says we need to find them all ponies and have them riding out each day. I shall speak to Mr Roberts about doing that very thing. I should have thought of it sooner. The boys need to be out riding!

We were all invited to the Tulridge's for dinner, only David and I went, leaving Fran to have an early night.

Blackie rallied today.

Weather – rain easing.

June 20th, 1863

Saturday

Oliver returned this morning just as we had finished breakfast. He and David talked for some time. It made my sore heart swell at the sight of them.

The boys were well behaved under Oliver's watchful eye. He did mention that he was taking Fran and the boys off for a week to the Scottish border. He realises that I (and David) need some peace from their games. They are the lights of my life but there are times when I ached for quiet. And he thought with Delia coming that the house would be very full.

How delighted I was to see Delia arrive this afternoon. My poor sister has aged terribly from this dreadful ordeal. Her hair is now nearly all grey, but it is to be expected considering what she suffers. The little children, two girls and one boy, (Cynthia, Iris, and Edmund) are all settled in the nursery with their two maids.

Mrs Higby is in her element having so many to taste her delights, she declares this is what she was born for - to cook for a large family!

I dread to gaze at the butcher's bill.

Blackie and Hollie aren't sure where to put themselves. So

many hands pat their heads all day, I'm sure they'll be bald before long. Blackie seems to have recovered whatever ailed her.

I was glad David retired early, such overwhelming days as today tire him easily. The shedding of tears is so exhausting, but it is happy I am to have my family under my roof. If Jonathan, Catherine, and Josephina were here, I'd be complete.

Weather - mild.

June 21st, 1863

Sunday

After church, the weather provided a warm day for the children to gallop around the gardens. A picnic was organised by David for the children on the clifftop. I can confess I did not rest easy with such inquisitive children wandering near the edge. It was with relief when all came home safely.

David feels better but is terribly thin. He and Delia sat in the sun in the orchard for a good time this afternoon just talking and sleeping. They both need to heal. One in body, one in spirit.

The house rings with voices and children's cries. David is bearing up under the pressure to be a supporting host as I deal with a grieving Delia. How my dear sister suffers. It is a cruel world where we have to bury our children.

All the excitement has brought Blackie down again.

Weather - sunny and warm.

June 22nd, 1863

Monday

Received a letter from Josephina and from Clementina. The former is enjoying the south of France, and the latter is recovering from a chest ailment, but also writes her brother Francis Sherbourne died suddenly last Thursday week. My dislike for Francis never wavered after his assault on me when I was 17, but I was sorry for Clementina who loved her brother dearly.

Also received a letter from Harry, stating his plans to take up the house (Briar Cottage) in the hamlet on the Monday following. I shall endeavour to have that house cleaned for his arrival.

Oliver and boys went fishing with David down on the shore. Fran, Delia and I sat on the terrace and did needle work while Mariana's children played with their nursemaids in the garden.

Such poor little dears, they hardly understand their loss. I fear the youngest baby, - Edmund – only 2 - will never remember his mother. And scarcely will the girls.

I recorded their names in the family bible as each child was born, Cynthia, Iris, and Edmund, but it was far too soon to add their mother's name and death date in the other column.

Blackie unable to leave her bed in my room. I am at a loss on what to do. David says it's kinder her to have her put to sleep, which means Mr Simons and his gun, but I cannot do it.

Weather- warm.

June 23rd, 1863

Tuesday

Another hot day. The children played outside until they were so tired, Nanny and Delia agreed an afternoon nap would benefit them.

David and Oliver took the boys swimming in the sea and were gone all day. They returned red-skinned and with salt in their hair, but with smiles as wide as their faces would allow.

Delia and I went for a drive in my gig. After a while I let her take the reins, but she was so slow I insisted on taking them back and urged Lolly into a fast trot, then a canter along the straight road near the church. Delia squealed like a child but in the end, we were laughing like of old. Friends of mine and villagers must have thought us mad as we cheerily waved to them as we passed.

Blackie tried to eat for me but was unsuccessful.

Weather – hot.

June 24th, 1863

Wednesday

Although we are in mourning, I spoke to Delia about inviting some friends to join us for a picnic on the cliff top on Friday. I feel Delia needs to be with other people, so her grief doesn't overwhelm her. It would benefit the children as well. She reluctantly agreed. Tomorrow I shall sent out invitations.

I know, only too well, how grief can define you if you let it. Losing Cole took away my identity. I didn't know who I was without him, without being his wife. Slowly, I regained my life, but only because my good friends and my children wouldn't allow me to wallow. I didn't want Delia to slid into that empty pit of sorrow. I know she cries her for daughter each night and her tears come easily when one of her grandchildren does something to remind her of Mariana. I feel I must do all I can to help her through this difficult time.

Fran is growing plump and well with child. Her sickness all but gone.

Today I bade the boys to write to their cousin Josephina, which after a grumble, they did. Arthur wrote such a beautiful letter, while Frank and Albie filled theirs with ghastly descriptions of gutting fish and catching a stoat in the wood.

I pressed some roses today, and a few pansies that have been drying in the greenhouse.

Delia sketched the children while David and Oliver took the boys to inspect the new horses Mr Roberts hired for them.

Blackie no better.

Weather - very warm.

June 25th, 1863

Thursday

Delia received a letter from Hamish, he is being posted to India. Delia is distraught and had to tell the children the news, but they are too young to understand. Hamish wants the children to accompany him out to that foreign land. Delia is beside herself. She will be losing not only her daughter but her grandchildren as well. Her heart is broken.

However, to offset that distressing news was the arrival of my darling Jonathan. Oh, how wonderfully well he looks and so like his father it brought tears to my eyes. I reprimanded him to never stay away from me so long again. I need his presence as much as I need Oliver and Catherine's. But alas, he has a wondering spirit. A spirit I think he inherited from me, and possibly David, (as a younger person I wished I was a boy so I could do the exact same thing as he's doing now.)

He has recently returned from his adventures in the West Indies. He has been gone for over a year, and it has been difficult for me to bear. But alas! He is here now, and that is all that matters. Jonathan overseas a lot of Cole's investments, one of which is a trading business between England and the West Indies. Still unmarried, my second son is in no hurry to change his single status despite having a good many young ladies eager for his proposal.

Many friends have accepted the invite to the picnic. I hope the weather holds.

Jonathan and Oliver wanted to take Blackie to Mr Simons. I selfishly said no.

Weather – warm with a sea breeze.

June 26th, 1863

Friday

The weather held, and the picnic was a success.

David seemed well today, but I noticed he rested on a blanket for most of the picnic. The little children ran and played games filling the air with squeals and shouts until they exhausted themselves.

Mrs Higby out did herself with multiple baskets of delicious cold meats, salads, jellies, cakes, and bottles of a variety of drinks. The two maids served us well.

We were a merry party.

Attendees:

David and I

Oliver, Fran, and boys.

Delia, and children

Jonathan

Jem and Regina Kilmore.

Walt and Enid Kitsen.

Don Lipton

The Reverend Jonas Tulridge and Fanny

Mrs Folkstone and her daughter Jenny

Mr Bains

Enid did do better today in hiding her feelings for David. I do feel sorry for her.

Sadly, when we all returned home, Mrs Clancey greeted me with the news that our sweet Blackie had died. Mrs Clancey had gone up to check on her and found Hollie sitting beside Blackie and when she checked, Blackie was no more. I am deeply upset by it. We'd had Blackie since she was a pup, nearly 15 years. My only comfort is she is in heaven with Cole - they are reunited. Jonathan, Oliver and the boys buried her under one of the apple trees in the orchard. I could not attend. I shall visit tomorrow and in the autumn, I shall plant some bulbs on her grave.

Weather – warm.

June 27th, 1863

Saturday

I am tired tonight. It is exhausting having the house full, but I wouldn't change it.

I have neglected my chores. My bookwork is terribly behind, luckily Mrs Clancey is very careful with the household accounts, and all shall be waiting for me when I do finally sit down to study them.

Oliver and Jonathan took the boys into Whitby for the day. They had the notion to maybe hire a small boat and take it out. Fran declared it a stupid idea as neither know much about sailing small row boats in a tidal bay. She lost the argument and apparently my little men had the most terrific time of it! They came home smelling of fish.

I spent much of the afternoon, after acquiring the keys for Harry's new abode, directing one of my maids in the cleaning of it while Mrs Clancey and I checked the sturdiness of the furniture and interview a hamlet girl for the position of being Harry's maid, and an older widow to be his cook. Both were successful in their actions of gaining the positions. I hope I did right by Harry who will arrive on Monday.

All this industrious work kept my mind from dwelling on Blackie until this afternoon when I went, along with Hollie, to place some cut roses on the grave. Mr Simons sent word that he will craft a handsome headstone for her, he is good with his hands that way.

Weather - fine.

June 28th, 1863

Sunday

Jonas gave a very good sermon and the values of charity, of not being afraid to ask for help when needed and in giving help when required as good Christians are meant to do. I hope that I am such a person as Jonas describes. Someone charitable. I strive to be.

To my shame I did not have a celebratory dinner in honour of the anniversary of Queen Victoria's coronation. Being so busy with the family it simply left my mind. We did raise a toast to her at dinner this evening. With the date falling on a Sunday, I am sure I shall be forgiven, not it is to the tower for us all! I shouldn't jest, but David filled my glass more than once tonight, will he ever act his age?

Hollie seems lonely without Blackie. I miss her as well. It is odd not to have her in my room at night.

Weather- very warm.

June 29th, 1863

Monday

Harry arrived complete with a wagon of baggage. We met him at his new house and helped him to get everything in. The boys enjoyed carrying the large trunks as though they were common labourers.

Harry was tired but pleased to have made it, along with his belongings, safely to North Yorkshire.

Invited out to dinner at the rectory tomorrow evening. David, Oliver, Fran, Jonathan, Delia and myself, plus Harry. Delia says she will not go.

I ordered Whitby jet mourning jewellery for Delia from W. Hamond. I still have my jet pieces I ordered for *my love's* funeral, and I wear them in honour of Mariana. I have shed my mourning clothes and wear dark grey which is an easier colour to accommodate this hot summer weather. No doubt our beloved Queen would despair of me for doing so when it's been such a short time since Mariana's death. However, I wore it for a year after Cole died and the starkness of the black reminds me of that awful time.

Delia remains in full black, as she should, but did not mind when I came downstairs this morning in my blue dress. Delia is in agreement that enough time has passed for me to wear colour again.

The garden is bursting with colour. It gives me such delight. Mr Perkins is happy with the kitchen garden and is daily harvesting produce for Mrs Higby. Every bit helps when I am hosting such a houseful of people.

Weather - hot and sultry.

June 30th, 1863

Tuesday

Harry has already had several people in the hamlet call on him about their ailments. I believe he will be just as busy here as he was at his establishment down south.

Letters from Catherine and Josephina – posted from Nice before they set sail to Italy. What an adventure they are having.

Don Lipton called - stayed for luncheon. He spoke about farming, which I paid full attention to, but it bored the others. I took pity on them and took Don for a stroll around the gardens.

Last day of the month. I spent most of the day confined in the study sorting through the accounts. Mrs Higby sat in with me for an hour before she left the bills for me to read. In the end my head ached from figures and Oliver finished the task for me. He is such a good son. He says I should be more strict in certain aspects of household expenditure, but on the whole, he was well pleased with my accounts.

Delia had endured another bad day of grief. At first, she cried off, saying she couldn't possibly go to the Tulridge's dinner, but David worked his charm and mentioned that Mariana would want her to attend. Then, Jonathan being the darling he is, brought her a flower from the garden and knelt down before her and read out a poem. At the end he said he would be her personal escort for the evening, and true to his word he played attendance on her all night. I'm so proud of him. I wish his father had seen him. We all enjoyed ourselves.

Weather - hot.

July 1st, 1863

Wednesday

Oh, such alarm today. My nerves are in shreds.

Firstly, David missed breakfast and when I went up to his room, I found him most out of sorts. A terrible fever upon him and any malaise brings him down so quickly with his various ailments and the lingering tropical diseases he's suffered from in the past.

I sent for Harry immediately. Harry insists David will not be in any danger for the near future if he rests and eats well. This of course he will, I shall make sure of it.

Fran has also remained in bed, she had a touch of bleeding which threw us all into a panic. Oliver read to her most of the day. Harry says Fran must stay in bed and not get up for many weeks. Delia is making it her mission to take care of dear Fran. I see the strain in her eyes as she gazes down on Fran and her mind thinks of poor Mariana.

Jonathan has offered to take the boys with him for a few days to Scarborough. Oliver agreed. They left this afternoon.

I am all at sixes and sevens. The house is all in a bother. Without Harry's quiet presence I do not know what I would do!

Caught up with my correspondence at last. I snatched an hour to write my letters this afternoon.

The weather is so hot. We need a storm to break the air.

July 2nd, 1863

Thursday

David still weak, I am truly worried.

Fran looking much better. Bleeding has stopped but Oliver refuses her to take one step from the bed.

Harry called twice today and assures me both patients are in no danger at present. He is in so much demand already, yet he always finds the time to come here, even when his own home and fireside awaits him. He stayed for dinner.

The house is quiet without my little men. Mariana's children are well behaved and stay with their nurses, mostly. Delia takes them for walks and teaches them about nature.

Enid Kitsen called with a basket of fruit for David. The news of David's illness has spread it seems. I told her he wasn't well enough to receive visitors. She stayed only a short time. Disappointment and concern on her face. A kind woman.

Weather - dry and hot.

July 3rd, 1863

Friday

Colour appeared in David's sunken cheeks. Blessed be to God. My brother seems to be recovering. He drank broth and ate eggs for breakfast. Harry was most pleased when he called. David sat in a chair by his window for most of the afternoon reading.

Delia cried again today. She received a note from her *detestable* husband demanding her return. The man is insufferable!

I have taken the step to write to him and explain Delia shall not be returning until her wellbeing is recovered from her tragedy.

David tells me to stay out of it, but I cannot. *That man* (Ian) may be her husband, but I am her sister, and I know out of the two I care for her more. Delia is in no state to return to the unhappy life she has with her husband.

Weather – storms brewing.

July 4th, 1863

Saturday

David insisted on leaving his room and coming downstairs for part of the day.

Jonathan writes that he and the boys shall return home on Monday, Fran is much cheered by this news.

Letter from dearest Audrey, they are now in London and shall be travelling to Yorkshire in a week. By the return address I sent her all information gathered about houses to let. I await her arrival with great emotion.

Blessed rain soaks the hot earth, but only for an hour. The storm came in wild and windy, drenched the parched earth for what seemed only moments and then blustered its way out to sea. The sky was spectacular with the colours of violet and green. Amazing to watch.

July 5th, 1863

Sunday

Only myself, Oliver and Delia attended church this morning. I pressured David to stay home. He is much recovered but sitting amongst strangers in church while he is still a little delicate would do him no good.

Fran is feeling much better and came downstairs for dinner this evening. Harry allowed it since the bleeding has stopped. Harry joined us.

Tuesday, we dine at the Kilmores'. Though I heard from another while at church this morning that Mr Kilmore's much younger brother is visiting them for a week. He lives in Edinburgh and is most handsome – an eligible bachelor. He has set the women of the parish all at a tremble.

Weather - hot weather has returned.

July 6th, 1863

Monday

Jonathan and the boys didn't arrive. We are all a little concerned as to why.

Harry called to check his patients. Later, we read together in the conservatory.

Delia and David went into Whitby. David said he must get out of the house or go mad. Delia accompanied him as I refused to consider him going alone until he is restored to full health. They were only gone a short time but enough to put David's mood in better shape.

Mr Don Lipton and Mrs Folkstone and Jenny called for afternoon tea.

Edith called and was disappointed that David was out, not that she mentioned it, but I could tell from her face. Poor woman, to be in love with a man who does not want you in return must be utterly dreadful. She must suffer so.

There was only ever one true love for me, but alas he is gone. In a vase beside my bed, his rose blooms beautifully, The Huntingdon Glow. My darling was so happy when he received his named rose for his birthday four years ago. I remember he told me it was nearly the best present he ever received, and when I asked him what was the best present ever, he gazed at me and said... *you*.

My heart does not beat properly without him.

Weather hot and windy.

July 7th, 1863

Tuesday

At last Jonathan and boys arrive. Horrid storms held them up on their last leg of the journey, so they put up at an inn. Fran is relieved and well. My son and little men seemed to have had a fabulous time exploring Scarborough. Jonathan is so good to have taken them.

Dinner at the Kilmores was interesting. Mr Kilmore's brother, George, was indeed as handsome as reported. He took an interest in me – possibly because he realised I wasn't yearning for marriage as some of the other women guests were. Poor man was inundated with offers of every sort of invitation from all parties. He will be much worn out after being here a week and entertained so thoroughly!

However, Mr George Kilmore seemed to enjoy most of the attention. And why shouldn't he? A single man with a fortune? He was like one of Jane Austen's delightful men in her books. I said the same to Delia, and she did laugh. It was good to see her smile.

Harry declared George Kilmore to be a self-serving kind of

chap. I did not agree for I saw no evidence of it. Harry was most put out and did not speak to me for the rest of the night. He was in an ill humour. But how could I agree when I didn't believe it?

I invited the Kilmores to a luncheon on Friday.

Weather – showery.

July 8th, 1863

Wednesday

Delia and David accompanied me to Whitby. Visited my seamstress and the milliners to collect all that I had ordered recently including a new dress for Delia – her horrid husband refuses her to have a sufficient dress allowance! I had also ordered some larger maternity clothes for Fran. She had brought nothing suitable with her for further along in her pregnancy and she is starting to show very well.

However! Oh, what a chore it was having David hover about in the shops and I declared to anyone within hearing that I shan't enter another shop again with my brother! David was totally insufferable, laughing and flirting with the stop-girls. He would put silly women's hats on his head and prance around in front of my acquaintances, much to Delia's delight, which only encouraged him. I was terribly ashamed of the pair.

I cut short or trip and came home in high dudgeon. I spent the evening writing my correspondence knowing I shall be the laughingstock of the town.

How I miss *my love*.

Weather cooler.

July 9th, 1863

Thursday

I called in at Mrs Peachy's residence for a short time (an elderly woman who lives in the hamlet. She is much an invalid and terribly lonely. Harry spoke to her last week and asked me if I would call on her.)

Then Delia and I had a drive to Mrs Folkstone's house for morning tea. Jenny was out – with Mr George Kilmore. Mrs Folkstone was abuzz about it. What may come of it, who knows?

In the afternoon Oliver and the nannies took all the children to the beach for a picnic.

David painted - to my wondrous joy he is painting the boys' portrait from a sketch he took of them secretly. The portrait will be hung in the library, I know the perfect spot above the leather chair where *my love* used to sit and read.

Delia, Fran and I caught up with our correspondence.

Jonathan went fishing and caught many. He was well satisfied. Mrs Higby changed the menu, and we enjoyed fresh fish. We all applauded Jonathan at dinner.

Weather – changeable.

July 10th, 1863

Friday.

The rain came down in torrents with enormous lightning strikes and loud claps of thunder which scared the smaller children terribly. I sent word to my guests to cancel the luncheon. Water was flooding across the roads, flattening the crops. A worry for the farmers.

Albie is in bed with a head cold, and I believe Arthur is trying hard to fight off the same symptoms. Fran is worried and is adamant the boys aren't to go near the sea again until all sign of illness is gone.

This evening, after the violence of the storms had passed out to sea, we had callers, Mr and Mrs Roger Marsh from Scarborough. He does business in London with Oliver and at Oliver's invitation called while he was in the district. They were a rather nice couple.

Harry called late. He was drenched to the skin. Been making calls on patients and was caught in the ugly weather. He dried off but was needed at a birth and was soon out in the drizzle again.

Weather – calming as the clock strikes midnight. I must go to sleep.

July 11th, 1863

Saturday

Arthur is looking better, and Albie is quite recovered.

The worried lines are nearly disappearing from Fran's face. Though she herself has been rather ill this morning, poor pet. She rallied by mid-morning but still looked peaky up until dinner.

I fear this confinement will tax her at her age. Her body has aged over ten years since her last birthing. I believe Oliver must keep her calm at all costs. I might suggest that she stay here when the boys return to school after the summer. I do know she feels their loss quite keenly and with Oliver busy with his interests, she spends much time alone so she might as well be here with me.

Inspected the gardens after the storm. All is well. Mr Perkins is such an admirable gardener. Always at his duties no matter the day or time or weather.

Letter from Josephina and Catherine. They are in Rome. Josephina sent a pretty sketch of the River Tiber. David was most impressed by it. Says she has talent. I completely agree.

Spoke at length with Mr Roberts (estate manager) about the plans for pending harvest.

David received a letter from our brother Sammy in Australia.

He invites us all out to him. This caused major discussions on the advantages and disadvantages of going, with no outcome yet decided. David is most keen for us all to go. Delia say Ian would never allow her to go. Ghastly man.

Harry was shocked when I told him about David's idea for us to travel to the other side of the world.

Weather - cool.

July 12th, 1863

Sunday

Reverend Tulridge delivered a most humbling sermon on the sacrifices made by Jesus for us. Jonas asked if we deserved it? When men war with each other and greed controls the world instead of love? What could we do to make the world a better place? We must start by making small differences to please Jesus. It was profoundly moving.

The day was cool and so the children stayed indoors, and David gave them all a painting lesson. His oils are nearly diminished from the activities. Albie's work was very impressive, but the younger children practised watercolour paintings, only I believe in some instances too much water was used, and the result was a very damp mess.

Delia was delighted by all the attempts and gave each child and kiss and a sugared almond. My little men were much impressed with the sugared almond, not so much with the kiss.

Weather – unsettled.

July 13th, 1863

Monday

Enjoyed a fine day and dried many flowers with the children's help.

This afternoon, Oliver took the boys off into Whitby to be measured for new clothes. They are growing into young men far too quickly.

Fran felt well enough to leave her bed for an hour and sat in the garden with us. Delia read to her while the small children played on the lawn.

Harry called and asked questions about our plans for Australia. I told him there were no plans made as yet. Harry was not pleased to see George Kilmore arrive and stay for afternoon tea. Mr Kilmore was most pleasant and entertaining. I do not understand Harry's dislike of the man.

Mr Perkins had informed me that rabbits had managed to get into the kitchen garden and eaten a great deal. This evening at dusk, Mr Simons, Oliver, and Jonathan took the boys rabbit shooting, with Jonathan saying it was his duty as Uncle to show them how to bag such pests. Albie shot his first rabbit. He was most impressed with his efforts. In total 5 rabbits are no more eating my vegetables! 3 rabbits are hanging in the cellar ready for the pot. I told Mr Simons to keep one for his supper and I gave the other one to Mr Roberts.

Won at cards tonight. David most put out. He does make me laugh, pouting like a schoolboy who has lost his ball.

Weather – warming up again.

July 14th, 1863

Tuesday

Oh, diary. What a deeply troubling issue that confronts me!

Harry called to say he would be away for a few days as he was attending a cousin's funeral in Manchester. I bade him to be careful and suddenly he quickly kissed me - not on the cheek as usual but on the lips, a lingering kiss!

I'm ashamed that he did so, and quite embarrassed. I do not know what possessed him, and I can honestly say I made him feel terribly upset by my shock and anger. He did not speak to me nor apologise but simply left.

I am at a loss to his actions. That he could break our friendship in such a way pains me more than I can bear.

I've sent him a letter informing him of my wish to not be in his company again until he has his emotions under control. No man has kissed me on the lips except Cole, (and that ghastly Francis Sherbourne).

July 15th, 1863

Wednesday

Extreme heat once more. Fran has remained in bed today as she fells most weak.

I felt quite misplaced throughout the day and cursed Harry for his actions once more. He has denied me our friendship for the rest of my life and for that I will never forgive him.

The family suspect I am upset at something but what can I tell them? They love and admire Harry so very much, as did I!

But this! It is too much for me to bear.

Later this afternoon, I set to weeding the garden, much to everyone's dismay at my frenzied attempts in the burning sun. Mr Perkins was beside himself at my endeavours which made him red in the face. He denied the weeds were of such an offence. I admit they were not. I found it difficult to find enough to take my frustrations out on.

At one point, Jonathan being the card he is, sat down beside me and helped. He told me funnies until I laughed.

Only afterwards in the quiet of the evening, Delia read out a poem that only days before Harry had read to me. It quite upset me.

I came to bed early to try and relieve my mind of its misery only I cannot sleep and sit here at my desk looking out over the moonlit garden.

Why did *my love* leave me? I miss him so very much. Does the pain ever lessen?

July 16th, 1863

Thursday

I slept hardly an hour all night and feel headachy with rising.

David heralded me into breakfast with non-stop chattering about Australia and us travelling there. I am in no mood for his games today.

The horrid hot weather kept us indoors and subdued. It was a day of short tempers and frayed nerves.

Jonathan's cheerfulness is a welcome relief. He and Oliver took the boys out riding.

Delia received a letter from her unpleasant husband that he is arriving tomorrow. I am livid that he comes here. Delia cried all day at her misfortunes, some of them I share with her but not her worst - *him!* She only has herself to blame in that!

I wrote to Audrey and cannot express enough my desire to see her shortly, I believe it will be any day. I would not be surprised if my letter was a waste of time.

Mr George Kilmore came to take his leave of us. I begged him to call on us again the next time he visited his brother. He replied that he would. What a charming man. I wonder if Jenny Folkstone is heartbroken at his departure? Mr Kilmore made no mention of returning to this part of Yorkshire again any time soon.

Weather – hot!

July 17th, 1863

Friday

Oh, that benighted man Delia married has arrived with two of his bibulous friends. The exhibition they made in the drawing room filled me with terror as one fellow was juggling my Wedgewood pieces! I believe they were all very sick with drink!

Delia fled in tears to her room, but I soon sorted her out and told her to show some spirit.

I told *him* to leave at once. He refused and promptly fell asleep in the library. In Cole's chair! The rudeness of the man!

David demanded that the two other men leave, and Oliver and Jonathan threaten such unpleasant things would happen to them if they ever returned!

Oh, what shame that *man* has brought to my house.

And now it is evening, and *he* is still under my roof and to make it worse David, Oliver, and Jonathan went riding this afternoon and then sent a note saying they were staying over at the Don Lipton's tonight. They obviously do not want to be in Ian's presence either.

So, I am alone, hiding up in my bedroom of my own house in

fear of meeting that *man.* I am most annoyed Delia married such an individual, why did Papa ever agree to it all those years ago?

It was indeed a most horrid day. I spent an hour with Fran sewing but my mind was not on it and then spent an hour reading to the children in the nursery. They were all out of sorts at the upset in the house.

Weather – overcast.

July 18th, 1863

Saturday

Such heat. I took all the children down to the beach for the morning to keep them out of the presence of that dreadful man, but they became red and hot and hungry, so we returned, and the smaller children were put to bed for a nap.

Fran was feeling much better and sat out under the large chestnut tree near the pond. I sat with her until the men returned from the Lipton estate and then left Olivier to keep her company.

Delia kept her husband entertained with a visit to Whitby. I care not what they did there.

To make it worse, today is *my love* and I's wedding anniversary and I am saddened to spend it without him. We married after I turned 18. We became engaged at Christmas 1820 and wed the following July. Oh, what a grand day it was! I had three attendants, Phillipa, Clementina and Delia (it would have been 4 if Maddy hadn't eloped and 5 if Felicia hadn't gone to Australia!). And everyone I knew was at the wedding to witness our love and joy. Papa said a speech at the wedding breakfast that made me and Mama cry, so lovely it was. I wore white silk with white tulle, ornamented with pearls and white lace. My bouquet was of pink roses and cream carnations.

We honeymooned first in London, at Cole's new house in Kensington for one night then travelled to Dover and from there we sailed for Portugal where we spent a week in Lisbon before another week in Cadiz in Spain. It was the best time of my life.

We returned to London, and that's where we lived and raised our children until Cole's retirement. How blessed I was to share so many years with him.

Earlier today, Oliver, and Jonathan, knowing what special day it was, both presented me with boxes of candied fruits and chocolates. The little men picked me wildflowers and Delia gave me a small book of poems by Blake. I am very fortunate to have such a loving family.

Weather – overcast but hot.

July 19th, 1863

Sunday

After church, Jonathan, and Oliver took the boys fishing, while David painted more on the little men's portrait. Fran, feeling very well today attended church for the first time in weeks. She and I walked about the garden, while Delia went for a drive in the gig with her husband.

This quiet summer's day ends with everyone well.

Weather – overcast but warm.

July 20th, 1863

Monday

Delia and I visited Don Lipton. While there Mr Lipton informed us that Harry had returned from Manchester and become ill with fever. I felt quite surprised by my reaction and at a loss over my intense fear for him. I told myself it was because he was a dear friend to me and would not wish him ill no matter what liberties he'd taken.

I felt very unwell at the thought of something happening to him, and my dearest friend joining my beloved Cole in the cemetery. Was Harry so ill that was possible? I did not know and fretted all day about it.

Of course, I cannot visit it him in case I carry the infection home, so I must remain wondering and praying. I have written to his housekeeper, Mrs Fernly, for news but as yet, nothing returns to me. I am most vexed at the lack of communication, but I understand she must be busy caring for the patient.

When he is well again, praise be to God, I shall certainly give him the length of my tongue for the amount of misery he has caused me lately.

Weather - cooler with grey clouds.

July 21st, 1863

Tuesday

No news of Harry by mid-morning made me drive the gig to Briar Cottage there I sat in the seat and called out to Mrs Fernly, Harry's housekeeper. The old woman came to the front step. She told me the good doctor was most ill and still abed. She looked worn and tired, poor woman. I asked if there was anything I could do, but she said I can only pray. I told her I'd send a basket and another maid to help her (for there is only her and one maid at the cottage). She was must gracious at the offer.

I came home most upset.

David tried to allay my fears, but nothing could dissuade the dreaded feeling within me of never seeing Harry again. How dare he get sick and worry me so!

July 22nd, 1863

Wednesday

On waking this morning, I quickly wrote a note to Mrs Fernly for news and received a note by return of my groom. Harry is still no better.

Later I went to church to pray for his recovery. Sitting in a silent church always leaves me peaceful yet today it didn't and on returning home I found the house in an uproar. Delia's husband was shouting at Delia, who was cowering behind a chair, and the children were upstairs crying. When I asked Delia what the problem was, that terrible creature she married turned on me and said Delia wanted to take the children to Hamish in India.

I replied that she should!

Oh, my what a terrible occasion it was. Jonathan and Oliver rushed to my defence when it seemed I was to receive that ghastly man's fist. Just in time he stopped himself from delivering a blow, though I know he has done so to Delia many a time throughout their awful marriage. My poor sister. My parents would be so distraught to see their youngest daughter so afflicted by such a man.

Jonathan and Oliver drove that disgusting man to Whitby to stay in a hotel there. He is not welcomed in my home ever again.

I pray for Harry's speedy recovery. I pray my sister finds some peace.

Weather – cool.

July 23rd, 1863

Thursday

This morning brought no news of Harry though I did send two notes by the way of the postman and my groom. If the house was empty of guests, I would instantly be at Briar Cottage, by Harry's side, but I cannot risk spreading the infection, especially to David, Fran, or the children.

Delia and that man she married went away for the day, I do not know where nor did I ask. Delia returned in the evening and remained in her bedroom until dinner. Thankfully Delia joined us in the dining room, but we did not mention *him*.

Fran joined us for dinner. She is looking so much better, and I am hopeful she is over the worst with this pregnancy.

Weather windy, ruining my flowers and brought a tree down in the park much to the excitement of the boys.

July 24th, 1863

Friday

Glorious news, Harry is over the worst as his fever has broken. Mrs Fernly wrote a note to me this morning, I cannot express my relief. I've sent another basket of fresh produce for her to give him the moment he is able to eat it.

On the opposite to this wondrous news is that Jonathan announced his departure. He is to leave tomorrow for the continent. He wishes to meet up with some friends in Paris and may join Catherine in Rome, which will delight her. Jonathan and she have a close relationship which he shares with Josephina too, and Charles – Catherine's dear husband.

I shall miss Jonathan terribly, but I understand his wanderlust need. I do hope he settles down soon though, I'd hate for him to remain alone all his life and miss the chance to have a great love like his father and I shared. I fear he is too much like David.

Fran is in great spirits as though her previous weakness never was. She and Oliver watched the boys play tennis on the lawn. She has eaten well and taken walks in the garden with the boys. They are delighted their mother is able to join them. They tell her such tales of fishing and hunting rabbits and swims at the beach. They are careful not to overtire her though and care so diligently for her when she is outside with them.

Delia's husband left Whitby this morning to return home. Thank the Lord. Delia is dithering on what to decide to do next, whether to stay here, go home, or travel to India to Hamish. I must be honest and say I am growing weary of all the children even though they are of the sweetest nature, and I have enjoyed their stay, but I am tired and long for some peace in the house again. I have spoken to her about the plan for India as I feel this is the best decision. Hamish is a good man, a good father and he will be overjoyed to have his children with him and Delia, who he adores. I told her plainly that if she takes the children to India, she will be free of that *man*. However, she feels duty-bound to him.

Another warm day and the garden is in need of rain. The roses and lavender still flourish but my poor potted plants are struggling in the heat. We have harvested a great deal from the kitchen garden, plenty of lettuce and tomatoes, cucumbers, and herbs. The fruit in the orchard is ripening wonderfully, but rain is needed to fill the water barrels, although the harvesting has started in some fields and the neighbouring farmers do not need rain just yet to hinder their efforts.

July 25th, 1863

Friday

Jonathan left, and I disgraced him with my tears, but I will so miss him, and he is so much the replica of his father that sometimes it hurts my heart to see him, yet for all that, I wish him well and made him promise to write many letters. I urged him to visit Catherine and I'm sure she'd be delighted to see her brother after so long.

Oliver travelled with Jonathan into Whitby to catch the steamer to London.

I sent some flowers to Harry to cheer his sick room. Plenty of roses. The flower being his favourite.

David amused the children for an hour playing hide & find. The house rang with laughter which tried poor Delia's shattered nerves. The best joke was Cynthia hid under Fran's bed and Fran played the innocent to it all while she sat on it and sewed!

Spent an hour at my writing desk replying to letters to many family members, including Clementina, Felicia, and Catherine and Cousin Philip.

No news from Audrey has me wondering what is holding her up from coming north?

I wrote a note to Harry, wishing him my best. I shall visit him tomorrow.

Weather - clouds build again but will it rain?

July 26th, 1863

Saturday

Fran felt most unwell today and remained in bed until the afternoon. She is concerned she has done too much recently, and my reassurances fell on deaf ears. If only Harry could come as he has a way of calming her like no one else can. Oliver worries and fusses and is no use at all. I sent him to Whitby with the boys to find some entertainment.

Spent an hour with old Mrs Reed at her cottage and took her some shortcake. She is bad with rheumatism.

Received a letter from Josephina telling me of her time in Rome. How I miss my little girl. She is so forward and bright and was Cole's favourite.

Took tea with Don Lipton. He had visited Harry the evening before and found him sitting up in bed and with good colour.

Had the Tulridges and Mrs Folkstone and Jenny to dinner. Jenny made no mention of George Kilmore. Apparently, nothing was arranged for them to correspond while he was away, or so she told Fran when we went into the parlour after dinner. Poor Jenny.

Afterwards, we played cards, at which I lost considerably, to David's amusement.

Weather – cool with grey skies.

July 27th, 1863

Sunday

Spoke to many people after church. There has been reports of several cases of cholera and scarlet fever up and down the coast. None confirmed in Whitby as yet. We must be meticulous in our ways to prevent the diseases from entering my home.

The war still continues in America, such a desperate situation for both sides, brother against brother, cousin against cousin. Oliver read out from the newspaper battles won and lost over breakfast. We hear of such new places, Vicksburg, and Gettysburg. It seems the North is winning the battle at the moment. I shudder to think of such bloodshed.

I postponed my visit to Harry at the last minute due to thunder, but no rain fell. I sent a note to Mrs Fernly asking after his health. Her reply sent back with my groom was Harry was in good spirits and recovering. I must be honest and say I am relieved to be spared seeing him for another day. I have no notion of what to say to him when we do finally meet. But I feel so sad to not have our easy friendship of before. Why did he kiss me?

Fran bled again today and must not be moved. (I can write such intimate details in this diary for no one will ever read it) She is very frightened and talks non-stop of stillbirths. It makes me shudder to just think it. I did take Oliver aside and remind him that at Frans age she should not have another baby after this one. It is too dangerous now. At six and thirty she should be allowed to be spared such dangers. They have three healthy sweet boys. This current child, should it survive, must be their last. Fran's health is most important. Fortunately, he whole-heartedly agreed.

Audrey did not arrive much to my disappointment. I watched out for her every hour.

Hollie hasn't been the same since Blackie died. I am worried.

Weather – much cooler, but no rain.

July 28th, 1863

Monday

Mrs Nell Watts, (a local councillor's wife) called for morning tea and was at a loss as to why I let the children roam the house. Even Cynthia's bouquet of wildflowers presented to her as she was leaving did not erase the scowl from her face. Poor woman never had children, and I believe enjoys her childless state. She has often declared children to be disease carrying much like rodents. I do not encourage her visits and rarely visit the woman myself. We do not have anything in common and the woman finds fault with everything and everyone. My beloved Cole didn't like her, or her blustery husband, and I shared his sentiment. I do not understand why she calls for I feel she is not keen on the duty. Perhaps she feels she should as an official's wife?

At last, this afternoon, Audrey arrived, due to many stops along the way to visit family. She and Reginald shall stay with me until their house is made up. How marvellous it was to see them, they looked so foreign with the golden skin, for Audrey is a keen gardener and spent many hours in the Indian sun much to her skin's detriment. She has bought me silk cloth in reds and golds, though of course I can never wear such things here in the north of

England, but I shall lay them over my bed and gaze at them each morning and night.

Audrey and Reggie have finally chosen a house on the edge of Whitby itself. It's not a large house, but one David and I visited. It consists of four bedrooms and small drawing room and sitting room, plus a dining room and servants' quarters. I am disappointed in their choice as others we visited were better, yet I could not be more delighted that she is but twenty minutes' drive from me.

Audrey greeted Delia with great sincerity and kissed her cheek many times in sorrow of Mariana. Reginald, dear Reggie, how I adore him, he's so big and bluff and laughs so well. Darling Cole would so love to have been here, and Reggie raised a toast to his dear friend at dinner.

Delia spent most of the evening asking questions about India, due to her own circumstances. Audrey and Reggie were very helpful in explaining the pros and cons of living on that continent. I feel Delia is even more confused and uncertain now. I believe in her heart she wants to go, but her horrid husband rules her.

We simply sat and talked until David started to snore reminding us that the hour was late, and we had days to catch up with news.

I sent another note to Harry telling him of my visitors and that I shall not know when I will have the time to call. (I am a most dreadful coward and feel utterly guilty. I am such a bad friend.)

So, now dear diary I shall close you and my eyes for it is nearly three in the morning and I must sleep.

July 29th, 1863

Tuesday

What a tiring day!

I had very little sleep last night, and the house is so full that Delia has decided to return home with the children.

To begin the day Audrey and I left straight after breakfast to do an inventory of the new house. Reggie went shooting with David and Oliver which gladdened us for we had no wish for him to trail our skirts while we made important decisions on the house's contents.

We returned at noon, laden with lists. It was as we ate Delia made her announcement. I hate the thought of her returning to *him,* yet she will enjoy having her own home again, I'm sure. She says she shall come back at Christmas if she decides to forgo India.

We had a frenzied afternoon of packing and sorting and lots of tears from the children, who do not want to leave, but to satisfy them I gave them each a kitten from the stables.

Tomorrow, they leave for the south and Oliver is to accompany them as far as York, for he travels to Manchester for business. He is taking Arthur with him, as the darling boy wishes to be a part of his father's world. Albie and Frank aren't so minded as yet. They, the sweet darlings, talk of nothing but being soldiers like they're great uncle Sammy. I have seen them both stare in awe at Sammy's portrait in full dress uniform which hangs in the hall.

It started to rain this afternoon, a refreshing rain which soaks into the dry earth, my flowers will be grateful even if the harvesters are not. I only have one more field to be 'brought in' then we are done for another year. Mr Roberts is most pleased with the bounty of wheat, barley, and hay we have stored in the barns.

I shall visit Harry tomorrow.

Weather – cool and overcast.

July 30th, 1863

Wednesday.

Thankfully the sun shone, and the rain departed.

After breakfast, we packed the hired carriages with Delia and children's belongings. Eventually they, and Oliver and Arthur took their leave of us at quarter past eleven.

I shall miss Delia and the children, but the house was needing a rest. Mrs Higby and Mrs Clancey are now able to let go off the hired servants we have had for the last few months, and I have promised not to hold a dinner party until Mrs Higby has recovered from the gout in her foot.

This afternoon, Audrey and I sat in the library and read our books. As we read, we listened to David and Reggie talk of the times when they were young men and of world events, the America war, which has affected the cotton mills in this country due to lack of cotton supply and also of the Māori rebellion in New Zealand. Why men must go to war is beyond me.

The two boys were sent to bed and Fran, of course, remained in hers. So, it was a pleasant evening of quiet reflection. However, I feel most dreadfully tired, and a little feverish. I think I need to sleep, though I must visit Harry and put this awkwardness I feel towards him to rest.

Weather – warm and windy.

July 31st, 1863

Thursday

I am beside myself with upsetment. Hollie, dear Hollie, has joined Blackie in a grave in the orchard. When I woke up this morning, she was in her forever sleep in her basket by my bed. Both dogs gone. I pray they are with Cole - I must believe that.

Audrey and Reggie said they would put off going to visit their new house to supervised the arrival of their belongings, but I persuaded them to go. The loss of a dog is personal. I did not want their plans to be altered because of it. Besides, I had Albie and Frank to comfort me.

In the afternoon I felt rather unwell suddenly. I was only able to write a few letters before I had to rest. Albie and Frank were very good and brought me hot lemon drinks and blankets. The weather remained grey and cool all day. They had the fire lit in my bedroom and that is where I have stayed all day.

Even now, I feel most ill. It makes me think of Harry. I must visit him.

August 11th, 1863

Monday

Oh, I am so remorseful to have missed so many days, dear diary.

My illness has been most severe. I am still abed and weak. Yesterday was the first day I could open my eyes and not have pain in my head. This evening has been the first time I could sit up in bed and hold my own teacup.

I feel most regretful to give my family such worry. Apparently, Harry left his convalescing to attend me, poor dearest man, but I was not aware of his presence or anyone else's for many a day. Scarlet Fever took me down into its Hell and tried to devour me. I give thanks to my return to the light and my beloved family.

Fran was ordered to stay completely to her side of the house, in the west wing, but she hardly leaves her bed never mind her room, so she was in no danger. David was sent to the Sea Dog Inn in Whitby to be safe, but after one night there, Mr Don Lipton rescued him and insisted he return home with him. Such a good man. Cole would have been proud of his friend's help.

But now I worry for the boys who attended me so well that first day. Mrs Clancey has assured me they are well.

I shall never be able to thank Audrey and Reggie for their taking control over the house while they put their own house plans on the shelf. What dear, wonderful friends.

Audrey has sorted out my correspondence into dates and sent notes to all invitations with explanations.

Now I am tired once more...

August 12th, 1863

Tuesday

Still weak but better. I shall get very few visitors until the fear of infection has passed. Audrey attends me most well.

David sent me a note saying he is well and for me not to worry. Don Lipton is looking after him exceedingly good.

From the door, Oliver sent his love. He has returned from Manchester only this morning. He tells me the boys are fine and hearty as is Fran who has left her bed to sit in the garden for an hour this morning. She wanted to attend me but was advised against it.

Harry came when I was napping, but didn't stay long. Apparently, the fever has taken hold in the area. He is awfully busy and not well enough himself to handle it.

I have much correspondence to answer but I tire easily.

Weather outside my window is rain clouds but still warm.

August 13th, 1863

Wednesday

Left my bed to sit by the window for a short time. I read my letters and reports from Mr Roberts and Mr Simons.

The weather has been extremely fine and warm. The harvest continues.

Audrey and Reggie spent some time away today sorting their house with new furniture.

Fran waved to me from the garden as I watched from my window. She is carrying the child high and other than being pale she is currently in good health. We must pray daily she stays so for the rest of her term.

The boys are well, and we think they may not have caught the sickness nor anyone else in the house.

When I am tired and weary, I long to join *my love*, but I soon shake myself out of that thought for he would be angry for me to leave our family. It seems it is not my time just yet.

Weather - warm and sunny.

August 14th, 1863

Thursday

David returned home today. He refused to stay away another day, bless him. He says Mr Lipton was a gracious host and we are in his debt.

Audrey sent notes to my friends telling them of my recovery. I have received bouquets of flowers and baskets of fruit daily for the last week. Audrey spoke to Harry while passing the hamlet. Scarlet Fever has cursed the area, and poor Harry is exhausted with the caring of patients.

I managed to find the energy to write to Delia, Catherine, and Jonathan, just a short letter to each. Afterwards I was most tired and slept for hours.

This evening David read to me after I finished my meal, but I was not much interested in his choice. He looked offended before laughing out loud and saying I would prefer Jane Austen or one of the Brontes' and I replied I would. He took up instead a book new to me that was most interesting. Elizabeth Gaskell's, *Sylvia's Lover.* Such a dramatic story and we shall continue reading it tomorrow. David is such a good brother.

Tomorrow, I shall venture downstairs. My accounts are so neglected and a sight to be seen!

Weather - fine. (from window)

August 15th, 1863

Friday

Fran and I sat in the garden for some time watching the boys play tennis. She is well today and while there is no bleeding she ventures outdoors for short periods.

I wrote to Harry but received no return note.

Oliver went to London today for a week. He has only been home a few days. The boys went with him to be fitted for new school uniforms. Oliver will also make arrangements for David's house to be packed up and sold.

David had wished to go too, but I persuaded him against it for going back to a dirty city such as London in the summer will do him nothing but harm.

David talked to Reggie a great deal about going to Australia to see Sammy, but I would not be drawn. Such discussion is tiring when unwell. I cannot think clearly.

No returning note from Harry made me ask David to call on him this afternoon. He returned saying the house was shut up. I am most worried.

Weather - windy but fine.

August 16th, 1863

Saturday

I felt much better today and collected my account books and worked on them in the garden.

The sun was very warm, so David had the wrought-iron table taken over and placed under the large chestnut tree. Here I worked in comfort, while sitting across from me was Audrey and Fran working on the library embroidery. David painted and Reginald read the paper to us.

Later, we had callers. My first in weeks. Mr Lipton and the Kilmores. I was most glad to see them and hear the latest gossip. Apparently, Jenny Folkstone also caught the fever but has recovered enough to be out of bed. There have been several deaths of it in Whitby, mainly the elderly and the very young. Such sadness. It was one of those most grateful days to be alive.

No word from Harry. I have decided to visit him tomorrow after church and this time I *will* go!

Weather – mild.

August 17th, 1863

Sunday.

Harry called. It was after church when I had just finished luncheon and was about to ready myself to take the gig to the hamlet. Audrey and Reginald had just left to visit their new house and assess when they can move in. David and Fran made their excuses from the parlour and so I was alone when he was announced.

We decided to walk in the garden. I could not speak, and I think he could not either except to ask after my health which I replied I was much recovered. We must have circled the garden twice before he stopped and picked a cream rose for me. He took my hand and kissed it and said he was sorry for his behaviour weeks ago. However, he announced his love for me was unchanged, that he had loved me from the first moment he met me when I was 17. He knew I loved Cole and was happy for me all these years to be with my wonderful husband, but he said that Cole was gone from this life and he wanted to know if I could ever love him. He wanted to marry me if I could consider it.

Before I had a chance to reply, he had walked away.

I stood on the lawn at a loss as to what to think or feel.

I am at a loss to understand him.

Oh, what am I to do? I wish I could talk to Cole and ask for advice but that would just be silly, for if Cole was here, there'd be no need for me to consider Harry... Oh, my mind is in a muddle.

Harry's actions quite ruined my day.

August 18th, 1863

Monday

Slept badly last night due to Harry's proposal, of which I have told no one about.

Audrey declared I need to have a change of surroundings. So, I accompanied her and Reggie to their new house. We spent the morning measuring garden beds with their new gardener, a young man with much enthusiasm. The house has been thoroughly cleaned and the new furniture put in place. They shall depart my home for their new abode tomorrow.

Received a letter from Jonathan. Darling boy is in Nice, and travels to Catherine shortly.

David finished the boys' portrait and what a splendid piece of art it is too. Fran cried on seeing the finished result.

Mrs Folkstone called at 3 without Jenny, who remains at home recovering. At 4 Don Lipton called and he and David went off for a ride.

Accounts are up to date, and I wrote to Sammy and Delia.

Harry plaques my mind and David's reading of *Sylvia's Lover* brought me no comfort.

Weather - beautifully warm.

August 19th, 1863

Tuesday

Audrey and Reggie departed this morning after breakfast. I am so pleased they are living close after 5 years of them being in India. Reggie's retirement and their decision to return to England, and more importantly to move to North Yorkshire, an area they have admired for years, gave me great comfort that Audrey would be close again. (They have come to visit us since Cole bought the estate when the children were little to escape the London summer. Cliff House was not only our summer residence but somewhere for Audrey and Reggie to visit also). Our longstanding friendship brings me such joy.

Audrey and Reggie's only child, Peter, is a solicitor and lives in London. He is unmarried and so there is no pull of grandchildren to sway them to return to London and Peter says he will visit often.

With the house so depleted of guests it prompted me to have not only the kitchen chimneys swept, but all the chimneys in the house as I did not have it done in the spring as usual. I heard that the sweep was in the village, so I sent word down to the man to ply his efforts here at Cliff House. He comes tomorrow. This action has instigated my orders for the servants to cover the furniture. Fran, feeling exceedingly well, and I forayed into the attics and found dustsheets for the stable boys to carry down. Mrs Clancey and the maids worked hard all day covering each room. They did a splendid job of it, and all is in readiness for the sweep in the morning.

I receive my taxes this morning to my disgust and shall have to venture to York soon to organise my affairs. I am thinking the first week of September to travel, but I have not truly decided. When I go, I will spend a day or two there and partake in a little shopping.

I am doing everything I can to not think of Harry.

Weather – mild.

August 20th, 1863

Wednesday

We cleared out of the house after breakfast because of the sweep working and instead went into the orchard and bagged peaches and apples.

Enid called and sat to watch us work which irritated David immensely, but I merely chuckled knowing Enid as I do. The very thought would never occur to Enid to actually stand on a stool and pick fruit. I believe she is of the type to not have an imagination. Stories of her childhood are awfully dull, poor dear.

More correspondence was my chore for the evening, though it is very pleasant to do so listening to Fran play the piano. Fran joined us for dinner and played chess with David. She won both games. David could not settle all night and his restlessness worries me. He mentions Australia too often.

What to do about Harry? I feel I should confide in someone but who?

Weather – much cooler. Rain started after dinner.

August 21st, 1863

Thursday

I have quite made up my mind to go to York on Monday instead of September. I feel David needs a distraction. So, he is to come with me. Fran is to stay home as Oliver and boys will be back on Sunday he writes.

Audrey and Reginald called and mentioned they are to travel to Scarborough for a week while some of the windows are repaired. Apparently, once they had moved in, they soon found to their horror that a majority of the upstairs windows rattle and leak – last night's rain revealed the weaknesses.

They stayed for dinner as it is David's birthday, and we had to celebrate it. Don Lipton also made a number at the table. Afterwards, we all played cards and David won which added to his pleasure of his special day. He was most appreciative of the gift I gave him of a book of famous artists. I had ordered it months ago.

I have not seen Harry at all, which vexes me greatly. He must explain himself for declaring himself. I fear our long friendship is totally lost. Insufferable man.

David and I have accepted an invitation for dinner tomorrow evening with the Tulridges.

Weather – rain and blustery

August 22nd, 1863

Friday

Visited Mr Bains for luncheon with David.

Spoke to Mr Roberts and Mr Simons, both are such good men and look after the estate exceedingly well.

Received a book of sketches from Josephina. So talented. David was certainly excited by them and says she must be tutored to expand on her natural abilities. I agree. David instantly wrote to Catherine.

This afternoon I wrote to Clementina, Maddy, Felicia, and Cousin Julian. It took me near three hours to do so and my hand was awfully stiff afterwards.

Mrs Clancey asked to speak with me. It seems the chamber maid, Mona is to be married in a month. I sent for the girl and gave her my congratulations. She is marrying a farmer from Robin Hood's Bay. We shall have to advertise for a replacement.

Dinner at the Tulridge's was very pleasant, surprisingly small in number which agreed with me very much. Attending was David, myself, and another couple I have not met before called Mr and Mrs Tyler. They come from Wiltshire. Mrs Tyler is a cousin of Fanny Tulridge. The Tylers' son recently arrived home from a trip to America. Hearing this, I mentioned the war and an enlightening discussion ensued about that country's plight at the moment. Apparently, the Tylers' son had a dangerous passage home as the ship had to run the American coastal blockades, such a frightening prospect is hardly worth thinking of. The ship was indeed shot at.

Anniversary of dear Papa's death. How I miss him. We are so far from Berkshire that I cannot put flowers on his grave. I did write and ask Delia to do so on my behalf should she manage to find the time to visit the graveyard.

Outside my window at this late hour, I hear the rain fall. The garden will be grateful.

August 23rd, 1863

Saturday

Oliver and boys returned home from London a day earlier than expected, bringing with them lots of presents and boundless energy. They have grown taller, I'm sure. How they delight me.

David and I took them down to the beach to give Oliver and Fran a moments peace and time alone.

I went for a long walk on the sand and thought of Harry's proposal. Despite the effort, I am still torn as to what to say to the man.

Weather - sunny and windy.

August 24th, 1863

Sunday

After church the boys played croquet on the lawn and Fran watched them from under the chestnut.

Oliver helped David and I organise our packing for the morning's departure. I am now excited to go. York is such a favourite of mine, and Cole and I spent many happy times there.

Later this afternoon, we enjoyed a picnic down on the beach. Oliver, the boys, and David fished while Fran and I read and talked sitting on a blanket. Fran much enjoyed having some time away from the house, poor sweet dear. How she has been kept at such close quarters with this pregnancy! She's been scared to leave the house and gardens for months.

The book that has caught my interest at the moment is *The Warden* by Trollope.

I have received no word from Harry. I spied him in church this morning, but before I was free from acquaintances he had gone. He does not know of the hurt he is causing me. I miss him terribly.

The countryside is in full flow of bringing in the last of the harvesting. Men, women, and children with their backs bent toiling.

Weather - warm but slight breezes.

August 25th, 1863

Monday

I write this entry from my hotel room. From my window the River Ouse flows by gently by, glistening in the moonlight. York is such a welcoming city. It is a feast for the senses.

We left Cliff House early this morning and travelled by train into York. Upon arriving, we selected our hotel and signed in. Once in the city, David seemed to spring to life like a flower after the rain. His enthusiasm touched me too, for within an hour of arriving we were eating lavishly at a restaurant and then David announced we were to go to the theatre, an occupation he much enjoys. Afterwards, we went to a small gathering hosted by a friend David was surprisingly reacquainted with at the theatre.

David enjoyed himself immensely. I know he delights in being with me at Cliff House, but society always claims a small part of him, and he withers if he's away from it for too long. I know he misses London very much.

It is very late, past 2. My feet ache and I am so tired I can barely see what I write. I am too old for such exciting entertainments.

Tomorrow, I visit my solicitor's office.

Weather - showery.

August 26th, 1863

Tuesday

Oh, such an exhausting day.

We spent the morning at the bank, the manager, Mr Wainstaff was so accommodating in regards to paying my taxes from my account, and it is a relief to have my affairs in order once more. After a lengthy visit to Mr Ramsgate, solicitor, I was able to have the afternoon shopping.

I bought two new hats for the winter and a new pair of cream soft kid boots, that button at the side. Then I bought two cashmere shawls, one for Fran's birthday and one for myself and ordered six new cotton petticoats, three linen chemises and lastly reels of coloured ribbons.

I bought new books for myself, Oliver and the boys and David replenished his art supplies. How busy we were!

Tomorrow I shall visit a seamstress and decide on a few winter dresses.

David found former acquaintances in nearly every street we stopped at (from his time living here after he finished university) and has invitations for the next week.

Tonight, we dined at the Forrester's, here in York. Stephen

Forrester is an old friend of David's from his Oxford days, and most attentive to me. He is a widow, with one daughter. He has invited us back again whenever we are in York. Such a lovely gentleman, and his daughter and her husband most agreeable.

Weather – cool and overcast.

August 27th, 1863

Wednesday

Today, we visited the museum in the morning and then enjoyed luncheon by the river.

In the afternoon, we spent time in a book shop, where I bought some piano music, and a book of poems to send to Josephina. Next, we toured an art gallery, and I bought a small oil painting of York Minster for my bedroom.

Tonight, we dined at a lavish restaurant. Then attended another theatre show at David's insistence. It was extremely loud and humorous, but I found it taxing. By midnight I was fighting my tiredness whereas David seemed to thrive. My brother is recapturing is youth, I'm sure.

Weather – fine with sunny intervals.

August 28th, 1863

Thursday

We went shopping again this morning, but as I spent so long in the dress makers, David went back to the hotel for a nap, as we were late getting home last night after our dinner and show.

I have ordered a new winter velvet gown in forest green with black lace around the neckline and hem. I also was most extravagant and ordered a fox fur stole and a new cloak with a fox fur collar and muff.

We dined in the hotel tonight as I refuse to go out again, after the late hours we kept last night and the night before. I can no longer keep up the pace I once was famous for. David went out. What a time he is having.

Weather – sun shining and blue skies.

August 29th, 1863

Friday

David went out alone this morning to visit an acquaintance living ten miles south of York. I expect him back tonight.

I engaged myself into writing letters, as I know at home a cluster will be awaiting my attention.

Later this afternoon, I took a pleasant walk down by the river. It was most peaceful and enjoyable. A small breeze cooled the warmness of the day, making it perfect to walk. It reminded me of the times Cole and I walked the very same path.

I am starting to miss my home. York is wonderful but busy, and noisy, and dirty. I require the calmness of my garden and to smell the sea air.

After eating dinner alone in the hotel, David returned. He changed and went out to meet with friends. He is enjoying himself greatly, but I fear his health will start to suffer.

I have been thinking a great deal about Harry and his proposal. I need to discuss it with someone. A few times, I have begun to speak of it to David, only to pull back at the last moment. I am in such a quandary. I feel I have lost my dearest friend, and I don't know how to fix things. One minute I am angry at him and then the next I am sad. What a position to put me in!

Weather – cloudy and cool.

August 30th, 1863

Saturday

Would have been dear Papa's birthday today.

This afternoon we had a picnic. We bought food and wine and hired a boat which David rowed upstream. After about a mile, we run the boat into a small shallow spot and scrambled up the bank like two children. Before us was a vista of waist high grass and fields of the last flush of wildflowers. It was so magical I cannot express my delight.

We ate, and explored, made friends with a cow and talked to a farmer we barely understood such was his strong accent, and lastly, we napped on a bed of daisies.

We returned to the hotel just as the sun was setting and not a more enjoyable day could be had. To make it perfect would have had *my love* with me.

David and I ate at the hotel and then I ordered a bath to be made up in my room. David has gone to meet friends. It is late now as I write. Such lazy days make one so tired.

Weather - gloriously warm

August 31st, 1863

Sunday

We went to hear the sermon at the Minster, but my mind kept straying from the prayers to look around at the magnificence of the cathedral. Such beauty took my breath away. I have been many times before, with *my love*, but this morning it feel so angelic to sit and wonder at its beauty as the sunlight streamed through the stained windows.

Afterwards, David and I went to the park and strolled for an hour before coming back to the hotel for our meal.

Later we went for another walk down by the river and then came back to our rooms to read and write letters.

We dined in the hotel this evening and so ends a quiet and peaceful Sunday.

Weather – a cool breezy day.

September 1st, 1863

Monday

This morning David and I selected a new rifle for Albie's 15th birthday, which is on Friday.

I also bought sugared mice for the boys, as well as a spinning top each. I bought a white silk scarf for Oliver for dinner parties in London.

I finished my letters and posted them. I am nearly all packed for our trip home in the morning.

We dined in a small restaurant in Petergate tonight but retired early for our journey tomorrow.

I am determined to speak to Harry on my return home.

Weather – rain.

September 2nd, 1863

Tuesday

We are home at last. We stayed away longer than I anticipated. I was very happy to see Oliver at the station waiting for us.

He assured us we were missed, and no mishaps happened while we were away and everyone is well.

It was a joyous welcome we received on entering the house, the boys were most jubilant and entertaining. Their embraces fortified me. I find that tonight I am most terribly tired.

Fran is looking well. I am very pleased.

It was the first time I've been away and not come home to Blackie and Hollie slobbering all over me with enthusiasm. How I miss my dear dogs, for as always, they remind me of Cole and his great love of them.

My little men helped me to unpack and were thrilled with their presents.

I have much to do tomorrow, and so I must sleep.

September 3rd, 1863

Wednesday

The number of chores that await my attention from being away just one week! I spent the morning at various activities which demanded my concentration. I had letters to read, invitations to reply to, accounts, servant requests and beside all this the boys followed my every move.

We celebrated Fran's birthday with a lovely luncheon and many neighbours called to wish her well. Audrey and Reggie are home from Scarborough, and it was lovely to see them.

Fran is blooming with health. She is large now and I pray nightly she delivers safely when the time comes. She was very taken with the cashmere shawl I gifted her.

Arthur read to me for a short time before dusk while Albie and Frank played chess.

Sadly, the boys and Oliver must travel to London on Friday. The boys start the new school term on Monday. Oliver wants Fran to stay here and have the baby. We all agreed it was for the best. Fran did not want to expose herself to the long train journey south – not when she is finally feeling so well. No one wants her to relapse before the birth.

Weather – cool. The trees are changing colour. Summer is gone for another year.

September 4th, 1863

Thursday

I was most surprised to find Harry waiting in the drawing room this morning as I left the breakfast room. I felt angry and cool towards him. At first, we spoke of nothing too intriguing until Harry suddenly started to pace the room. I was quite put out by this display and asked him to explain himself. He again professed his love to me. I was speechless. I could feel the warmth leave my face at his words.

My lifelong friend saying such things to me held me immobile.

Harry then went on to inform me of his love which he has cradled within his heart for far too many years. His bachelorhood is tenement to me. Out of respect for my love to my husband, he has kept quiet since Cole's death, but he wishes to know my heart on the matter. He cold wait no longer for an answer. Such an announcement irked me out of my stupidity, for I would not take the blame for his lonesome state. I did not ask him to remain unmarried because of me.

I ordered him out of the house and requested that he not come again unless he was more in control of his thoughts and emotions.

At my time of life, I am unable to be charitable to his fancifulness.

His visit put me into a temper all day and I begged everyone to leave me alone. I spent the day in my room reading Cole's love letters from so long ago.

I am most distraught.

September 5th, 1863

Friday

Albie's birthday was every reason to be joyous, and I tried valiantly for his sake, but my heart was tortured because of Harry. Albie was surprised and most grateful for his new rifle, which shall be kept here in the gun room with Cole's guns.

Audrey and Reginald came bearing a gift for the birthday boy, and we ate cake and no end of wonderful treats. I confessed to Audrey in a quiet moment of Harry's disagreeable behaviour, but she simply shook her head and said I was being foolish to be so affected.

She went on to tell me I would find no better a husband than Harry, a trusted friend, and that I should not have to spend the rest of my life alone.

I emphatically explained that I was far from alone, with my family in attendance most times, but Audrey told me there was a difference.

I do not understand her. Even before David came to stay, I had plenty of entertainment and a busy life. I made it busy after Cole's death so that I could simply *live* without him. I never thought to love again.

No one seems to understand my suffering and Audrey isn't aware of how I feel so keenly of Harry's betrayal. I have lost his friendship that I valued so highly.

After luncheon, Oliver, and the boys departed. Fran was most upset. We shall see the boys again at Christmas. Oliver will return soon for the arrival of the new baby.

The house is eerily quiet with just myself, David and Fran. I decided to host a dinner party next week and wrote out the invitations after dinner. I did not invite Harry.

Weather – much colder than we've had in many months.

September 6th, 1863

Saturday

We woke to a light shower that soon turned into a steady rain.

With the weather so inclement I did not expect any visitors and was amazed when Harry was announced into my sitting room, where I was reviewing my autumn plans for planting as guided by Mr Perkins.

My traitorous heart skipped a beat on Harry's entry, and his shy smile made me want to slap it from his face. He came and knelt in front of me at my knee like a servant to a queen, and I felt myself blush like a young girl in the nursery.

I will never forget his words.

My dearest, Beatrice, you were the girl who stole my heart, and you became the woman who I placed above all others, so that no other lady of my acquaintance could possibly compare. You may shun me, you may forbid my presence, but you cannot halt my love.

His words made me cry. I cannot try to describe my thoughts or feelings even now at this late hour.

After his declaration, Harry begged me to think over our long friendship, of his love and finally of a future together.

His parting words were, *if I could not see us spending the rest of our lives together then he would rather be dead.*

Can I possibly lose another man who means so much to me?

I have loved Cole for so long, even death cannot separate us, I will not let it, but I admit that Harry helped me through that terrible time and without him in my life I would not be so happy, but to cross over into matrimony? Just the thought fills me with betrayal towards Cole.

Oh, what to do, what to do...

September 7th, 1863

Sunday

I spied Harry in church today and I was quite upset by my nervousness. I found no solace within the holy walls. Afterwards, I quickly made my escape much to David's confusion. Audrey invited us to afternoon tea tomorrow, but I refused gently. I need time alone.

The coolness of the day made me restless. I spent the afternoon walking the sands below the cliff. I am in turmoil.

September 8th, 1863

Monday

Audrey called for she knew I was suffering from some inner turmoil. I told her what Harry had said to me. She thought him a lovely man who could make me happy if I let him. Then she said we should take some air and put my worries aside for a time.

We visited two of my estate tenants. Unfortunately, I was much too troubled to pay proper attention to their concerns and begged to go home. Audrey was alarmed at my behaviour and said I could not go on with this problem. Before she left she asked me truthfully if I loved Harry, and if I did, then I should do something about it. She told me that Cole would want me happy.

I thought of myself to be already happy.

I cried off visiting friends. I could not be in company today.

I spent the afternoon with Fran. She was having an uncomfortable day, and I soothed her by reading to her. For a short time, I made myself think of nothing, but the words written in front of me.

This evening, I refused to play cards with David. He harangued me at every opportunity to tell him what ails me, but I cannot. What can I say? I escaped to my room.

I will never forgive Harry for crossing over the boundaries of friendship.

September 9th, 1863

Tuesday

I pray for some easement to my pained heart.

This morning, roses arrived with a note, *love Harry*. I had the urge to smash them against the wall, but Fran and David were watching. The light breakfast I had managed to swallow threatened to erupt. I am too old to be tortured this way. Harry had no right to turn my life upside down like this.

I kept my mind occupied with visit to Mr Simons and Mr Roberts and the later I visited Mr Bain and the Tulridges.

I spent the evening writing to Delia, Jonathan, and Catherine.

Weather – pleasant.

September 10th, 1863

Wednesday

I received two invitations for dinner next week, and I am inclined to decline both. I have my own dinner party on Friday, and I am close to cancelling it. I am not in the mood for company.

David watches me closely and is annoyed I do not confide in him what obviously troubles me. How would he understand such things?

Has he spent most of his life with just one person, only to have that dearest person taken from them before they were ready to part?

No, he has not. He has never married, and the one woman he did propose to, declined him and married another. David simply doesn't understand my problem.

At lunch we were interrupted by Harry's arrival. I was shocked at the sight of him. He had lost weight and looked older, as though he hadn't slept for many nights. I felt a spark of satisfaction at that. I wanted him to suffer as I had.

I know I was cold to him, and I left David and Fran to entertain him. After a short time, Harry, and David went walking out to the cliff, I watched them go from my bedroom window.

When David returned, he was alone. He found me in my study working on the accounts and didn't disturb me. An hour later he knocked on the door, however, I was discussing menus with Mrs Higby, but I dismissed her and beckoned David to enter. He came to sit opposite me and after a moment he took my hand between his two.

He told me Harry had confessed his love for me to him, but he of course already knew of it. David told me he knew Harry has loved me since before I married Cole.

This annoyed me. Had did I not know?

David felt I should give him an answer yes or no and be done with it, but I explained nothing is so easy and he agreed.

Next, he astounded me with a plan.

He wishes to travel to Australia. He was utterly serious. He says if I do not accept Harry, then I should go with him. He believes Sammy needs us. I was surprised at this, and David went on to explain that a recent letter from Sammy mentions his loneliness. Sammy has a longing to see his family but has been unwell and cannot travel.

I spoke of David's own health on undertaking such a long and exhausting journey, but he replied that Harry recommends a sea voyage would do his chest good.

I cannot leave my home to travel to the other side of the world at my age. I told him so. He rebuffed my excuses. Stating that friends and family members of ours have travelled the oceans into their nineties. But I know I cannot leave Cliff House. Cole is here. His presence cloaks the house, evidence of him is in every room and can be seen outside from every window.

I will not leave him.

September 11th, 1863

Thursday

It is the anniversary of Mama's death. How can I still miss her at my age, when I have children and grandchildren? I miss her no-nonsense ways. I could always rely on her to think sensibly. I always felt she looked at me as if I could and should do better. Yet, the memories that come to play in my mind today have been ones of beauty. I remember her dressing for a ball, I believe it was the night of my first ball. How magnificent she looked, and how Papa admired her.

David and I laid flowers at the village church altar in memory of her. She is buried far from us, with Papa in Berkshire, but this mark of respect makes us feel closer to her real grave.

As we left the village, we passed Harry. He had been out all night at a birthing, he looked tired and unwell. He said both mother and child had died, and he could not save them though he had worked for hours to do so. In that moment I wanted to climb from the gig and go to him, but something inside me stopped me and then the moment passed.

We continued on as thunder clouds rumbled in the distance. David took me to task all the way home for making Harry suffer so. He did not stop with voicing his thoughts until I yelled at him to halt the gig and let me down. I marched off into the wood at the edge of my estate.

It began to rain not long after and I was thoroughly wet by the time I reached home. David met me in the hall and apologised but we were interrupted by Mrs Clancey coming down the stairs at an alarming pace, white-faced and speaking fast. David calmed her, but her words had me rushing upstairs to Fran. Dear Fran has been suffering pains since midnight but has quietly borne it without complaint.

I sent for Harry immediately.

He came within the half hour. We did not speak of anything but Fran. David went to Whitby to telegraph Oliver. Fran still has at least six weeks to go to full term. Harry is worried her age and the time between births will make this birth difficult.

It is now 1 o'clock in the morning and I must try to sleep for I shall be needed when the birth starts in earnest. Harry gave Fran a sleeping draught to ease her, hopefully the pains will lessen and perhaps stop. It could be a false warning. I pray it is so.

Harry sleeps in the spare room and David is sitting beside Fran and is to wake us both should Fran need us.

Weather – overcast.

September 13th, 1863

Saturday

I am so tired.

Friday is a blur to me I remember little of it, and today is the same. (My dinner party was obviously cancelled.)

I have been sent to bed for an hour's rest, and I do wish for it, but I feel guilty to close my eyes even for a second as Fran still suffers. Poor dearest Harry can barely stand such is his exhaustion of attending to Fran after his previous patient. He has had very little rest between each birth. David keeps him supplied with food and drink. He encourages him to go outside for fresh air, me as well, but it so difficult to leave poor Fran who is terribly brave dealing with such terrible pain.

I know Harry worries whether there will be a good outcome, and his doubts echoes in me.

We all pray for a safe deliverance of a healthy child, and I pray harder for Fran to come through it well for she is a mother and is needed by her boys.

It is times like theses that I miss my own mother, who was so supportive when I had my own children. Fran's own mother died a few years ago and she only has me to be at her bedside.

Audrey has been the best of friends taking care of my household while I stay beside Fran.

Weather – cool.

September 14th, 1863

Sunday

This morning at five minutes past eight o'clock, Fran gave birth to a tiny little girl, so small that her head fits into my hand perfectly. Fran is weak but not bleeding badly. She sleeps now after consuming some tea and toast. Oliver, who arrived late Saturday, is with her now.

Harry has gone home. David has driven him as the poor man is so tired he can barely stand from exhaustion.

This afternoon, I slipped out to visit the church, to offer my prayers of thanks for the safe delivery of Fran and the baby. On my return home, I saw Mr Perkins waiting for me at the end of the drive. He had picked flowers for Fran. How sweet of him.

As I sit here, from my bedroom window the setting sun is throwing long shadows across the lawn, and beside me in the white and lace cradle sleeps my granddaughter. She is of good colour, with a tuft of dark hair. Her skin is so fine I can see her minute veins beneath.

Cole would be joyous to see and hold her, he so loved babies. I remember when Oliver was born, Cole held him for the first time and cried such happy tears. From that moment my love for him soared to a place it never came down from. With each of our babies' birth he would come to me straight afterwards and kiss and hold me so hard I thought he would snap my bones.

As I look down on my granddaughter now, I ache for his arms to hold me again.

I have spent the evening writing letters to family of the news, including the boys to tell them of their new baby sister.

Weather – calm.

September 15th, 1863

Monday

My granddaughter is to be called Hope Beatrice Victoria Huntingdon. What a name for such a tiny person.

So far, she has fed well and sleeps a great deal. Fran insists on feeding her herself, and I am pleased, for I fed my babies, much to my mother's disapproval. Cole supported me entirely, even if the conversations and arguments with my female relatives embarrassed him until he flushed the shade of a radish.

Oliver is still anxious about both Fran and Hope. Harry's visit today eased him some, as Harry thought that Hope showed good signs of survival. After feeding her little stomach was as tight as a drum and this made us all smile.

With the upheaval of the last few days, we missed raising a toast to Albie on his thirteenth birthday, although he is at school.

We have decided on a small dinner party for Friday to celebrate the safe arrival of Hope. Fran is worried that we shouldn't celebrate Hope's arrival yet for she is so small she could still have difficulties, but Harry persuaded her to overcome her doubts. Hope is here, alive and so far, in good health. Her arrival should be celebrated, and a long life must be toasted to her.

I have sent invitations to close friends, and Oliver has sent an advertisement of Hope's birth to his friend who is an editor of *The Times.*

This evening, I have written so many letters my hand hurts, I will continue more tomorrow.

Weather – rain and cold.

September 16th, 1863

Tuesday

The last few days have been exhaustingly busy. I have barely found the time to see to my own personal affairs as I care for Fran and the baby, but both are doing very well, and I feel more confident that they will both continue to flourish.

Harry has called every day. He is the most kindest of men and so considerate to me and my family. However, we skirt each other like fighters in the ring. Unsure of how we want to treat each other and fearful of saying the wrong thing.

I have come to one momentous decision however, and that is I *will* travel with David to Australia to stay with Sammy for a year. We shall leave in a month's time. A month will give us the chance to organise everything and by then Fran will be back to her normal self and need me less and will return home to London with Oliver.

Now I have made the decision, am I keen to see Sammy. He has been gone a long time from the bosom of our family since taking up soldiering as a young man. I am excited to see where he lives and learn much of the country that sits so far away from us on the globe.

David is as excited as a dog with two tails now I have agreed.

He has written this very day to Sammy and to a friend of his who owns a clipper, a fast-sailing ship that makes the journey to Australia and back quite often carrying wool. David has requested passage as soon as possible. Apparently, these types of sailing ships can make the journey from England to Australia in just 80 days or so depending on weather. David tells me the clipper is the better option than going by steamer which must stop several times to take on board coal. I shall leave the exact details to David. Thankfully, I am a good sailor, so I do not mind which ship we take. That said, the faster we get there and be with Sammy, the better.

I have yet to tell Harry of the decision.

Made calls to Mrs Folkstone and Jenny and the Tulridge's.

Audrey and Reggie came to dinner, along with Don Lipton. We raised a toast to the newest member of the family. David and I announced our news of travelling to Australia. Poor Audrey cried for nearly half an hour at the idea of it. I do feel very bad to be leaving her just when she has moved here. She understood, however. She had done the same to me when they went to India and left me in London. My dearest friend realises this is what I need and wishes my all the luck. She promised to host a huge party when we return. Bless her.

I have written to Cousin Felicia and told her our plans, since she is in Australia and the ship stops at the port in Melbourne, where she lives. With luck we should be able to meet her there before we sail on to Sydney.

Weather - continued to rain.

September 17th, 1863

Wednesday

Mrs Fernly has sent a note that Harry has taken ill. He has caught a fever from one of his patients and possibly because he has been so exhausted of late. The poor man has worked harder in this hamlet than he had in his practice in the south! Mrs Fernly says he is not dreadfully bad but needs to rest, which I completely agree with!

I have a megrim from the worry over him and how excitable David is with all the plans he's making. He is like a child at times. I sent him to have dinner with Mr Bains in Whitby. No doubt afterwards they will visit a local inn and drink themselves stupid as men are wont to do!

Fran and baby continuing to do well.

Weather – rain clearing.

September 18th, 1863

Thursday

I have been attending to Harry for the last day and a half. He is recovering now but gave me such a scare. To see him weakened and listless gave me such a terrible worry. I thought of how I would feel if he were to leave this world, and I knew I would be heartbroken.

I must reflect on what these emotions mean and how I should deal with them.

I still have not told him about going to Australia.

Fran and baby doing very well.

David's house in London has sold. He is well pleased with the result. He has made a tidy profit, enough to finance his lifestyle for the rest of his life. I spoke to Oliver about selling some of our London properties, not our home there where Oliver and his family live, but other places Cole bought years ago, and we rent out. Oliver said to wait as we are not in need of the money such sales would bring.

Weather is much colder. The trees are such beautiful colours of gold and reds but are quickly becoming bare.

September 19th, 1863

Friday

I sat with Harry for most of the day as he refused to stay in bed and had to come downstairs. His home is comfortable at least, for a bachelor. Mrs Fernly, his housekeeper, is clean and honest and a good servant to him.

I read the newspaper to Harry, then we had morning tea. Afterwards, he insisted on going for a short walk and it was while we were walking that we discussed my forthcoming journey. Harry was upset to be losing my company for nearly 2 years.

I bade him to take a nap once we returned, but he refused, saying that he had little time left with me and would not waste it by napping. We sat in front of the fire in his parlour and ate a light luncheon meal of pea and ham soup and fresh bread with a platter of fruit to finish.

I made my leave at 2. My heart was heavy, knowing I had caused Harry anguish with all this Australia business.

At home, all was in preparation for my dinner party. The last of the summer roses decorated the dining table, and Mr Perkins had harvested the last summer vegetables in the garden for Mrs Higby.

I went upstairs to sit with Fran and the baby until it was time for my bath. I dressed in one of my new dresses made in York.

My guests arrived at 7 and we made a large party.

Attendees:

Myself, David and Oliver

Audrey and Reggie

Reverend and Mrs Tulridge

Mrs Folkstone and Jenny

Mr and Mrs Kilmore

Don Lipton

Mr Bains

Mr and Miss Kitsen

Harry did not come, stating he didn't have the strength for socialising, and I agreed. He needs more rest.

David and I announced our travel plans to the rest of party who didn't already know them and were congratulated and asked many questions.

Weather – cool and breezy.

September 20th, 1863

Saturday

Called in to see Harry. He is much improved. I stayed for morning tea and told him all about the party the night before. He asked after everyone, especially Fran and the baby. I could happily assure him everyone was in good health.

He then asked me if I the plans to travel to Australia were definitely in place. I said they were close to being completed once David received word from his friend with the clipper. I did not like witness the pain on his face at the thought of me leaving for so long. I took my leave of him soon after.

Received a letter from Delia. She has decided to go to India. I am so thankful she has come to that decision. Her ghastly husband forbids it, but Hamish has organised it all. Delia and the children will leave in secret Friday next. Imagine having to escape in secret from your own husband! But that is her life being married to such a detestable fellow!

I will not have the chance to see her before she goes, which upsets me greatly, but David says we might be able to visit her on the way to Australia or at least on the return journey home. This reassured me greatly. I wrote to Delia straight away and told her all our plans. God willing, we shall see each other soon.

I have written to Jonathan and Catherine about my travelling to Sammy. I suggested that was it possible for them to continue on to Australia as well? I would be utterly ecstatic if they could. Catherine's husband, Charles, is a very wealthy man, and he has no need to be in England, hence their long expedition through Europe. If they could venture to Australia and we could be together, that would bring me such happiness. Jonathan's plans may not support such a trip for I know he has business elsewhere he must oversee.

How far-flung my beloved family is and will be in the future.

I will be sad to leave Cliff House for what could be for 2 years according to David's calculations. But I have very good staff. I entrust Cliff House and the estate to Mrs Clancey, Mr Roberts, Mr Simons and Mr Perkins completely. Audrey and Reggie said they would call by often and Reggie will be the first person any of my staff will contact should the need arise. I have given Reggie full responsibility, which will keep him happy in his retirement for he was fearful of growing bored with nothing to do. Not now! Now he will have two households to oversee, Audrey as well. They said such responsibility will make the time go by much quicker.

I will miss Oliver, Fran, and the boys and Hope, and of course my dear Harry and all my other friends. However, I feel now is the time to do it. I am doing it for Cole, who always wanted to go to Australia. I am doing it for David, who also needs this one last quest before his health fails him. I am doing it for Sammy, who has gone years without seeing familiar loved ones. And I am doing this for myself. One more adventure before old age takes my ability to enjoy such things.

Weather – cool but with sunshine.

September 21st, 1863

Sunday

A very vexing day!

This afternoon when I went to visit Harry after church, I found one of Harry's neighbours sitting with him having tea. The woman, a widow by the name of Jane Valentine, was acting very familiar towards Harry. Topping up his teacup, offering more of her freshly baked shortbread. She spoke that she and Harry often share a daily cup of tea when Harry's work allows him the time. And apparently, many a time Harry has gone to her cottage and had dinner with her. Just the two of them. This was all news to me! Harry has never once mentioned the woman.

Well, I cannot explain my manners, for I believe I was rather rude and told Jane Valentine that Harry was far too busy to be *monopolised* by one particular friend! And that he was *most considered* by a *great many people* of the area, and she should not expect to have him all to herself!

I left in rather a temper.

When I returned home. I told David what had happened, and he had the audacity to laugh at me. He told me it was my own fault if Harry had been singled out by other women. I had refused Harry's love and so why shouldn't another woman have her chance?

I was mortified by his words. How dare David make fun of me?

September 22nd, 1863

Monday

I am to be married.

Oh, my!

It has happened so quickly that I do not know what to make of any of it.

Let me explain myself.

Harry called this morning immediately after breakfast. He wanted to understand my behaviour yesterday.

I refused to apologise for my actions towards Jane Valentine. Then I surprised both myself and Harry by asking him to come with us to Australia.

Even now, hours later, I do not know what possessed me to utter those words. Only, I realised I did not want to spend over a year or more without him in my life.

Harry took my hand. He said he could not be without me and if David was in agreeance he would travel with us.

I cannot express how happy that made me.

Harry asked me if I could ever think of him as a husband. I lost my thoughts and my speech for some minutes and then realised that yes, I could imagine him as my husband. I did love him.

For so long I had cared for this lovely warm and kind man, but my grief of losing Cole held me in a such tight grip for a long time.

I have relied on Harry for all things. I wasn't being fair to him to keep him just as a friend when he wanted so much more, and my emotions, my reasoning, when I finally understood my own thoughts, confirmed that I also wanted more than simple friendship from him (especially after seeing that horrid Jane Valentine fawn all over him!).

Truthfully, and I can be truthful in my own diary, I miss being loved by a man, of being held and adored by someone, just as I missed giving my love and devotion to another, of sharing secrets, of whispering hopes and dreams – even at my age.

Since Cole's death I never expected to feel this way again. Cole was my everything, my world, my anchor. However, I finally understood that Harry wasn't replacing Cole. Instead, he was simply adding a different richness to my life that I so desperately ached for and didn't know it.

We are to marry in three weeks with David, Oliver, Fran, plus Audrey and Reggie, and all our friends present to witness our happy day. The following day we will travel with David to London and from there journey to Southampton to sail for Australia.

It seems ridiculous at my age to be excited again like the young girl I once was, but life is too short to step away from the chance of experiencing more adventure and love.

How lucky am I?

Goodnight, diary. I confess this will be my last entry. I shall purchase a new diary in London to chronicle my next journey in life.

Beatrice Charlotte Acherton Huntingdon (soon to be Hylton)

About AnneMarie Brear

Author of over forty novels, AnneMarie Brear has crafted sweeping historical fiction with atmosphere, emotion and drama aplenty that will surely satisfy any fan of the genre. AnneMarie was born in a small town in N.S.W. Australia, to English parents from Yorkshire, and is the youngest of five children. From an early age she loved reading, working her way through the Enid Blyton stories, before moving onto Catherine Cookson's novels as a teenager.

Living in England during the 1980s and more recently, AnneMarie developed a love of history from visiting grand old English houses and this grew into a fascination with what may have happened behind their walls over their long existence. Her enjoyment of visiting old country estates and castles when travelling and, her interest in genealogy and researching her family tree, has been put to good use, providing backgrounds and names for her historical novels which are mainly set in Yorkshire or Australia between Victorian times and WWII.

A long and winding road to publication led to her first novel being published in 2006.

She has now published over thirty-five historical family saga novels, becoming an Amazon UK best seller and with her novel, The Slum Angel, winning a gold medal at the USA Reader's Favourite International Awards. Two of her books have been nominated for the Romance Writer's Australia Ruby Award and the USA In'dtale Magazine Rone award and recently she has been nominated twice as a finalist for the UK RNA RONA Awards.

AnneMarie lives in the Southern Highlands of N.S.W. Australia

http://www.annemariebrear.com

Printed in Dunstable, United Kingdom

78324272R00231